No Second Chances

The shot had come from just to the left of the engine on the roundhouse cradle.

Longarm moved to his left just in time to see the shooter's back as he ran out the other side of the roundhouse.

Longarm took a gamble . . . ran around the north side of the roundhouse and grunted with satisfaction as he saw the gunman scramble into sight . . .

You lose, Longarm thought to himself as the shooter, seeing Longarm standing in front of him, skidded to a halt, slipped on the loose gravel and cinders, and almost lost his footing.

"Drop it," Longarm shouted. "You're under arrest."

Instead, the gunman, a panicky look on his face, raised his pistol in Longarm's direction.

Longarm triggered his Colt and then again. His first bullet took the man low in the belly, doubling him over and dropping him to his knees. The second probably would have struck in the same place as the first except that by then the gunman himself was lower. The second slug slammed in to the top of the man's head . . .

LONGARM

AND THE
MARK OF THE CAT

J
JOVE BOOKS, NEW YORK

THE BERKLEY PUBLISHING GROUP
Published by the Penguin Group
Penguin Group (USA) Inc.
375 Hudson Street, New York, New York 10014, USA
Penguin Group (Canada), 90 Eglinton Avenue East, Suite 700, Toronto, Ontario M4P 2Y3, Canada
(a division of Pearson Penguin Canada Inc.)
Penguin Books Ltd., 80 Strand, London WC2R 0RL, England
Penguin Group Ireland, 25 St. Stephen's Green, Dublin 2, Ireland (a division of Penguin Books Ltd.)
Penguin Group (Australia), 250 Camberwell Road, Camberwell, Victoria 3124, Australia
(a division of Pearson Australia Group Pty. Ltd.)
Penguin Books India Pvt. Ltd., 11 Community Centre, Panchsheel Park, New Delhi—110 017, India
Penguin Group (NZ), 67 Apollo Drive, Rosedale, North Shore 0632, New Zealand
(a division of Pearson New Zealand Ltd.)
Penguin Books (South Africa) (Pty.) Ltd., 24 Sturdee Avenue, Rosebank, Johannesburg 2196,
South Africa

Penguin Books Ltd., Registered Offices: 80 Strand, London WC2R 0RL, England

This is a work of fiction. Names, characters, places, and incidents either are the product of the author's imagination or are used fictitiously, and any resemblance to actual persons, living or dead, business establishments, events, or locales is entirely coincidental.

LONGARM AND THE MARK OF THE CAT

A Jove Book / published by arrangement with the author

PRINTING HISTORY
Jove edition / November 2010

Copyright © 2010 by Penguin Group (USA) Inc.
Cover illustration by Milo Sinovcic.

ISBN: 978-0-515-14857-2

JOVE®
Jove Books are published by The Berkley Publishing Group,
a division of Penguin Group (USA) Inc.,
375 Hudson Street, New York, New York 10014.
JOVE® is a registered trademark of Penguin Group (USA) Inc.
The "J" design is a trademark of Penguin Group (USA) Inc.

PRINTED IN THE UNITED STATES OF AMERICA

10 9 8 7 6 5 4 3 2 1

Chapter 1

Custis Long sighed, dipped a hand into his pants pocket, and placed a nickel onto the counter next to his empty coffee cup. He did not have to pull out his key-wound Ingersoll to know that he was late. He was. Again. And he had been full of such good intentions when he woke up this morning.

Still and all, he thought, glancing down toward the far end of the counter, the new waitress was definitely a cutie. He would have to pay some attention to her. Give it a week, perhaps two, and he was thinking that rounded little ass would be bouncing on some mattress quite nicely.

"Come again, sir," he heard behind him as he swiveled around on the café stool and reached for the flat-crowned brown Stetson he had placed on the stool next to his.

The tall, dark-haired deputy United States marshal pretended not to hear, not wanting to be too quick to become friendly. A touch of bad-boy mystery, he had found, often worked wonders with the weaker sex.

The man known by lawman and lawbreaker alike as Longarm was a study in brown. Brown hat, seal brown hair and mustache, brown tweed coat, brown corduroy trousers. But low-heeled black cavalry boots and black gunbelt strapped around a narrow waist. He strode out the doorway, open to the refreshingly cool morning air, and turned toward Denver's Colfax Avenue and the Federal Building where Chief U.S. Marshal William Vail had his offices.

Longarm hustled up the stone steps he had taken so very many times over the years and headed down the corridor to a door with a frosted glass panel and over it a transom that was never left open. There were secrets spoken of inside that particular office, and gaping transoms were an invitation to eavesdroppers. Newspapermen, for instance, or, worse, defense lawyers. If there was anything Custis Long could not abide it was a damned defense lawyer.

He stepped through the door and removed his hat. Without bothering to look up from his desk, Billy Vail's chief clerk, Henry, grumbled, "You're late."

Longarm shrugged. "Sorry." Which he was not. "I had to lay some charm on a new waitress."

Henry looked up from his paperwork. There was something . . . Longarm could not be sure, but he thought there was a . . . a sparkle, that was it. There was a sparkle behind the polished lenses of Henry's spectacles. "The boss wants to see you."

Longarm tossed his Stetson onto the elkhorn hat rack and said, "You wanta tell him I'm here?"

Henry shook his head. "Go on in. He was expecting you fifteen minutes ago."

Longarm quickly scrubbed the toe of each boot over the back of one of his calves, tugged at the back of his tweed coat, and adjusted the string tie at his throat. There was no need, but old habit made him touch the grip of the double-action .45-caliber Colt that rode in a cross-draw rig just to the left of his belt buckle. That item without fail was placed precisely where it needed to be. Finally he smoothed down the handlebar mustache that accented the sun-darkened crags of his face.

"What are you doing, Longarm? Trying to make yourself pretty? I really don't think it will work."

Longarm glanced back at Henry and glowered, not really meaning it. Then he lightly knocked twice, turned the knob, and entered Billy Vail's office.

"Late again, I see," Billy Vail said by way of greeting. Vail was seated behind his desk, a clean-shaven, pink-faced, round-cheeked man in a gray business suit. Vail looked more like a bookkeeper or a clerk than a former Texas Ranger who had brought in more outlaws and survived more gunfights than most people had ever read about.

"Sorry, Boss," Longarm said. He still did not mean it.

"Sit down," Vail invited.

Longarm took the indicated chair and leaned forward. "You got some work for me?"

"I do, Long. Something very, um, special." There was something in Billy's voice. Longarm could not put his finger on just exactly what, but . . . there was something.

"Just give me the warrants an' point me where you want me t' go, Boss."

"There are not any, um, warrants."

Longarm's eyebrows went up.

"I need a favor from you."

"Sure, Billy. You know I'm always ready t'do a favor. If I can, that is."

"Yes, well, that should not be in question. I just need for you to, um, deliver a package."

"All right. I can do that."

"Of course you can. And the recipient will be right on your way to Omaha."

"I'm going to Omaha?"

"That's right. I want you to pick up a prisoner there. A Delbert Schrank."

"Never heard of him," Longarm admitted.

"I wouldn't expect you to. Schrank is small potatoes. He pilfered some stamps from a post office in Wyoming. He will be brought back here for trial in federal court."

"For a few postage stamps?"

"For that and to put pressure on him to tell us what he might know about the Jennings gang. We think he is friendly with Jennings's brother Matt. If Schrank has a choice between talking with us or going behind bars for five years, we think he will roll over on his friend."

"Jennings," Longarm repeated. "I've heard of that one."

"We want him. Schrank may be the way to get him."

"You say he's already in custody?"

"That's right. The Omaha chief of police has him. At least one of his patrol officers pays attention to the wanted posters. He found Schrank enjoying a beer at a honky-tonk there and brought the man in."

"Lucky for us," Longarm observed.

"Yes, it is."

"You said you want me t'deliver a package on my way there?"

Vail seemed to squirm a little in his high-backed swivel chair. He spun it around to face out of the window, then turned the chair back to face his deputy. "Not exactly a package," he said.

"All right. It ain't exactly a package. Whatever that means. So what exactly is it?"

"It is, well, it is a cage?"

"A cage, Billy? What, are you wantin' me to deliver a bird or somethin'?"

"It's not a bird. It is, um, a cat."

"A *cat*?"

"My wife had a visitor. Her oldest, dearest friend from her childhood. The woman is terribly attached to her cat, but while she was visiting, the cat slipped out of an open window and disappeared. She looked everywhere but finally concluded that the cat was gone forever. After she resumed her travels, we found the cat. My wife bought a cage for it and wrote to her chum with the good news. Now we need to return the animal to its owner. She, the friend I mean, wouldn't trust just anyone to take care of her precious pet, and my wife, uh, prevailed upon me to come up with a solution."

Billy leaned back in his chair and smiled. "You, Custis, are that solution."

The boss looked, Longarm thought, rather like a cat himself at that moment. One that had just caught a canary.

"Henry has all the details for you," Billy said. "Now, if you will excuse me, I have to meet with someone over at the courthouse." He stood and smiled again. This time Longarm was fairly sure he could see canary feathers peeking out of the corners of the boss's mouth.

"Good luck, Custis."

"Yeah. Thanks. I think." Longarm got out of there before Billy could think of something else for him to do.

Chapter 2

"You ain't gonna believe what they're wanting me t'do now," Longarm mused as he idly petted the back of Sheila Mixon's head. She at the moment was engaged in sucking Longarm's cock, so she could only mumble an answer of some sort.

"They want me to escort a damned cat to Nebraska," Longarm grumbled. "A cat! I ask you."

Sheila disengaged from Longarm's towering erection and looked up at him. "I love cats," she said.

"Well, I don't." He grinned. "But I sure as hell do love what you're doing down there." He lightly touched the back of her head and encouraged her in the direction he wanted her to go.

Sheila kissed the flat of his belly, then resumed blowing him. She took the head of his cock into her mouth and swirled her tongue around it. Around and around and around some more. Longarm loved that particular sensation and Sheila knew it. Finally she settled down to some serious sucking, drawing his dick deep into her mouth until it reached and quickly entered her throat.

Between the tight ring of muscle and cartilage at the upper reaches of Sheila's throat and the compression of her lips at the base of his cock, plus the pressure of her tongue pushing hard against his shaft, Longarm was overwhelmed with pleasurable feeling. His body stiffened, his eyes drooped shut, and a low moan escaped from his lips.

Sheila continued her delightful assault on him for only a few sweet moments before the storm clouds gathered deep within Longarm's balls, both pressure and sensation building until he could contain them no longer. A jet of hot cum shot up through his prick and exploded into Sheila's throat.

She kept him inside her mouth, pulling back just enough so that she had only the bulbous head still there and applying strong suction until the last drops of living sperm were taken into her mouth and swallowed.

"You taste nice," she said as she released his dick and came up to cuddle at his side on the narrow bed they were sharing.

"An' you give one helluva blow job, lady."

"Thank you, kind sir." She smiled.

Longarm bent his head and kissed her. The taste of his own cum lingered in her mouth, a warm and slightly salty flavor. His probing tongue encountered hers and the two thrust and parried inside Sheila's mouth.

His hand found her right tit. He squeezed and felt as much as heard Sheila's moan of pleasure. He squeezed harder and she abandoned his mouth to toss her head back and cry out.

"Yes," she hissed. "More."

Longarm took her nipple between thumb and forefinger and applied pressure until she trembled and whispered "yes" yet again, her voice husky and low.

"Take me now, Custis. Take me, please."

He levered himself on top of her as Sheila opened her legs to receive him.

She gasped as he thrust deep inside her, the head of his dick hammering her cervix with each forward push. Her pussy clamped tight around him, and he could feel the rising intensity of sensation within her body.

She began to quiver and thrash her head back and forth on the pillow beneath her, and her hips pumped wildly, her belly slamming hard against his.

Longarm's own pleasure mounted, rising inside his balls and streaking outward in another explosion of juice, the fluids perhaps less this second time, but the pleasure reduced not at all.

He stiffened on top of her and felt Sheila's own burst of orgasm, her flesh clenching hard around his cock and her belly fluttering and pulsing as wave after wave of sensation swept through her.

After long moments she relaxed. She pushed him off of her, and as Longarm rolled over, Sheila grinned and muttered, "Damn, Custis. Damn but that's fun. Wanta do it again?"

Longarm chuckled. "Give me just a minute to recover here, girl, and we'll see what happens."

"I'm game, Custis. Anytime you say." She reached down and gently tweaked his half-limp pecker, then her hand crept down warm and soft to cup his balls and simply hold them.

Longarm sighed and stroked Sheila's back, enjoying the soft, smooth feel of her skin. After a minute or so his flagging prick once again began to rise. Sheila let go of his balls. Her fingers circled his cock, and she began to move his foreskin up and down as if she were trying to jack him off.

"Mm. Nice," he mumbled.

His cock began to fill out to its full, firm erection.

"What were you saying, Custis?"

"Did I say something? Oh, yeah. Damn cat. I hate cats. But not now, baby. We'll talk about this later." He rolled on top of her, and again Sheila spread herself open to him.

Chapter 3

He pondered taking a hansom to Billy's house but hesitated when he thought about it. This was not actually duty-oriented. It was a personal favor for the boss. "The boss's wife" would be more accurate. Henry was sure to raise a fuss if he put the cost of a cab on his expense account, so this was very likely to come out of Longarm's pocket. Or Billy's ultimately, except Longarm would be ashamed to ask the boss for reimbursement.

No, better to travel on the cheap and forget about the price.

Longarm walked across Cherry Creek and on to Colfax Avenue. There he stepped onto a westbound streetcar, paying the nickel out of pocket. Billy's house was located just a few blocks from the streetcar line.

Once he reached the Vail home, Longarm let himself into the yard and mounted the steps onto the porch. He removed his hat and slicked his hair back with the palm of his hand, then stroked his mustache and twisted the ends before he rapped twice on the door.

No one came, so after a few minutes he tugged the bell-pull. That brought an answer.

"Coming." The sound came from somewhere far from the vestibule. Moments later the inner door was pulled open and Billy's wife could be seen through the partially frosted glass of the outer door. She smiled when she caught sight of him. "Custis. How lovely to see you, dear. Come inside, please."

Longarm carefully wiped his boots—there was no mud or dirt on them, but habit is a strong master and hard to break—then stepped inside, feeling something like a kid tiptoeing in among the grown-ups. Billy's wife always seemed to have that effect on him. She was a perfectly nice woman, and there really was no reason for him to feel like that. But he did. Every time he saw her. "Ma'am." He bobbed his head and shifted his Stetson back and forth from one hand to the other.

Mrs. Vail looked like she was dressed for a garden party. Despite that she was wearing a frilly apron over her garments. She had a smudge of flour on the tip of her nose. It bobbed very, very slightly whenever she spoke. Longarm found the thing beyond fascinating. He wanted to reach up and wipe it off but contained himself. He knew the lady, but not *that* well. "Ma'am," he mumbled again.

"Oh, good heavens, Custis. Relax. I won't bite."

"No, ma'am."

"William said you would come by this morning to pick up Sam."

"Sam, ma'am?"

"The cat, Custis. My friend Cleo's cat. The one you will be taking to Wansley. In Nebraska?" The last came out sounding very much like a question, as if she were beginning to doubt him.

"Yes, ma'am," he said quickly. "Can I ask, uh, where this place is? I never heard of it."

Mrs. Vail waved her hand as if the question was of no importance. "It's somewhere over there. She said it is small. She has to drive over to Fullerton to find a telegraph so we can communicate."

"Fullerton," Longarm repeated. "Yes, ma'am. You, uh, don't happen t'know where Fullerton is, do you?"

"Oh, you can find it. Just ask someone."

"Yes, ma'am." The instruction obviously was simple to her. Go to Nebraska. Ask directions to a place called Fullerton—at least it was large enough to have a telegraph station—and then to this Wansley town, village, whatever. Simple.

"I have your instructions already written down for you. I suggest you commit them to memory." She handed him several sheets of paper fixed together with a large pin, probably a hat pin.

"Yes, ma'am."

"Come this way, please. Sam is in the parlor."

Longarm dutifully followed where the lady led. He stepped into the parlor. And stopped short.

The birdcage he was supposed to transport to Nebraska was just plain huge. It could have contained a vulture. Hell, it would have held a mating pair of them.

What it did hold was indeed a cat. A cat that was black as the devil's heart. It was past being big. Sam was a monster. Fat. Surly. When Longarm approached the cage to take a look at the animal, it hissed and drew back into a crouch.

"This is, um, Sam?"

"Yes." Mrs. Vail smiled. "Beautiful, isn't he." She stood next to Longarm and the cat relaxed its posture. Mrs. Vail opened the cage door—Longarm almost stopped her for fear the damn cat would claw her—and reached inside. Sam crept forward and rubbed his forehead over the back of her hand, then rolled onto his back so she could scratch his belly. Longarm was not sure, but he thought the grossly overweight beast was purring.

"I know you will take the very best care of him." She fetched another sheaf of papers from a side table and handed them to Longarm. "These are the instructions as to what Sam eats. He must be fed daily, of course. Several times would be better. And his sandbox. He is very particular there should be no sticks or other objects in his sand. Clean builder's sand is best. I packed a small supply for you to start with, and I'm sure you can find more along the railroad. The sandbox must be emptied daily, of course, and the sand replaced with fresh."

She smiled.

Longarm did not.

"Yes, ma'am" was all he could say.

But *damn* Billy owed him after this.

"Pardon me, ma'am, while I go find a cab t'carry me and Sam over to the Overland depot." He had originally thought to carry an ordinary birdcage in one hand and his trusty old carpetbag in the other. Hell, he would be lucky if he could lift this monstrosity of a cage. And that was without the monstrosity of a cat inside it.

Longarm set his Stetson carefully onto his head and touched the brim as he dipped his head in a slight bow toward the boss's wife.

Lordy, what had he gotten himself into this time!

Chapter 4

Longarm settled gratefully onto the hard slats of a railroad depot bench. He was close to being worn out, first by having to walk for miles and miles—seemed like that much anyway—to find a conveyance that would carry both himself and the cat cage, and then by wrestling the damned thing onto the roof of the cab and into the depot afterward. He did not know for sure how much the beast weighed. Twenty pounds. More. And the cage was no lightweight. Worse, it was large and ungainly, with no proper handholds. The terrified cat banging around from side to side did not help either.

"Two dollars and seventy-five cents for the freight, mister," the freight agent had told him. "You'll want to get off at Grand Island. Have to take a coach from there. Fullerton is, um . . . let me check my map . . . Fullerton is north and a good ways east from Grand Island. There ought to be some sort of road though."

"Thank you." Longarm paid the man out of pocket again.

"You should arrive in Grand Island tomorrow at 11:20 P.M."

Longarm frowned. A late evening arrival meant he would have to sit in the damned depot until morning, when he might be able to catch a coach to this Fullerton place. From there . . . it was anybody's guess how he could get the cat from Fullerton to . . . what was the name of it . . . Wansley. He really should have told Billy to shove it up his ass when the boss asked for this favor. Still, he was in it now.

"Want a ticket for yourself, mister?" the ticket agent asked. "You will be traveling with that thing, won't you?"

"Yeah." Longarm sighed. "I'm afraid I will." He pulled out his wallet, but instead of searching for money to pay for a ticket, he displayed his badge. "But I won't be needing a ticket, I think."

"No, sir. I didn't know," the railroad man said quickly.

Federal agents, including deputy United States marshals, rode the federally subsidized rails, also on any stagecoach lines that carried U.S. mail, without charge. Longarm supposed he could have jawboned the damned cage onto the freight car without charge, but he just would not have felt right about that. It wouldn't be proper for the railroad to pay for Billy Vail's favor.

Not, he realized, that the railroad would be out of pocket to carry a few more pounds of freight. But still and all . . . he just would not have felt right about it, and though Custis Long might—indeed frequently did—bend the rules at times, it was always to make something right. He never did it for his own benefit. Better to pay the few dollars than to feel like a piker.

Since he would have to visit the freight car now and then to tend the cat anyway, for this trip he tossed his carpetbag onto the baggage cart along with the cage, then helped a porter trundle the awkward cart down the platform to the open door of the appropriate car.

The cat was hissing and yowling the whole, bumpy way.

Longarm couldn't say that he blamed the beast. It was probably accustomed to being carried on a feather pillow by an adoring mistress.

Between himself and the freight handler they managed to muscle the cage aboard without too seriously bending any of the heavy gauge wire bars. Longarm tossed his bag up into the car too and asked, "How long till we pull out?"

"Twenty minutes. Maybe more."

He nodded and went off in search of a pail of drinking water. Down here in the city you had to be careful where you drank. Assuming you wanted to drink water instead of something more interesting. Up in the mountains you could pretty much drink water wherever you found it. Well, with the exception of drain-off water that had been used for processing minerals. That could well include acids or arsenic, and either one of those would ruin your day. In the city, found water could include any sort of shit. Literally.

Inside the depot he located a bucket that claimed to be good water, had a dipper full of it himself, then looked around for something to carry it in. In the trash he found a discarded metal can that originally held Georgia peaches. He filled that from the pail and carried the can back to the freight car.

"Something wrong, mister?" the freight agent asked.

"No, just bringing some water to the cat there."

"All right, but be quick. We don't allow passengers to ride back here. I'm not making an exception for you."

That was a bunch of shit, and Longarm knew it. Passengers transporting favored dogs or horses or bulls or any-damn-thing else rode the freight and livestock cars all the time. All he said though was "I'll be gone in a minute."

"See that you are."

The agent's insistence made Longarm curious, but it was not his business. He did, however, wonder if there was something the man wanted to hide. Something he would be doing while the train was under way.

Longarm poured his can of water into the little bowl Billy's wife had provided inside the cage, bowls for both water and food actually, and got his hand the hell out of there double quick. The cat was not hissing any longer, but the hair on the back of its neck rose, and Longarm thought the cat was about to attack him. Damn beast!

"When's the next stop?" he asked.

The freight agent just shrugged. "Scheduled stops at Fort Morgan and Sterling. End of the line at Julesburg. In between there's a dozen places where we might be flagged down."

Longarm nodded his thanks and headed for the platform, where he could enjoy a cheroot—and a look at any traveling young ladies—until the conductor called for passengers to board.

Chapter 5

"Up one." Longarm shoved a silver dollar into the small pile of coins in the middle of the table.

"I'll see that and raise you five," the fat man said. He was a drummer from Cincinnati and a nice enough man but a lousy poker player. Whenever he got a really good hand, he tugged at his shirt collar as if to loosen it. He was tugging at the collar now.

"Getting' serious now, are we?" Longarm mused.

The next man to the right stared at his cards for a little too long, then shrugged and tossed them in. "Too much for me," he said.

It was a casual pickup group of men in the smoking car. They had been playing for the better part of three hours. Longarm was down a few dollars but not enough to worry about. They had played through the Fort Morgan stop. Longarm needed to go see to the cat, but the beast could just wait a bit.

"Up to you." The drummer prodded the bespectacled little man to Longarm's right.

"I think . . . I'm out." He too folded and sat back in his

chair. He pulled a plump cigar from inside his coat and began the process of trimming and lighting it.

Longarm was in a mood for a cheroot too, but it could wait.

"What about you?" the fat man asked, looking at Longarm.

"Your five and fifteen more." Longarm dropped a gleaming yellow double eagle onto the table as the railroad car swayed and gently bumped its way east across the plains.

The fat man blinked and sat up straighter. He had not expected that, not after Longarm drew three to an obvious pair. He thought for a moment, then said, "All right. Your fifteen and, um, twenty-five more." He dropped two of the handsome gold coins into the pot.

The gent obviously assumed that Longarm had three of something, and whatever that was his hand could beat it. Longarm, however, had unexpectedly pulled two queens to match the pair of them he already held. And four queens would be hard to beat.

"Call." Longarm contributed his own double eagle.

The fat man grinned broadly and spread his cards on the table.

One minute later Custis Long was ambling back through the coaches, his pockets satisfyingly heavy with other people's money. He nodded a pleasant hello to the conductor and passed by, then had a thought and turned back again.

"Excuse me. Sir. Wait a moment there, would ya please."

The conductor stopped and waited for Longarm to join him.

"Could you help me with a couple things? I have some coins I'd like to change for bills if you have 'em. An' I need something to carry water in. An empty bottle or a pitcher. Most anything will do. I got a animal back in the baggage car. I expect it needs some water."

"I'm sure I can find something for you, Deputy, and I can change your money if it isn't too much."

Longarm dug into his pocket and handed over his winnings without bothering to count them.

"Wait here."

Longarm followed the man as far as the open platform between cars and stopped there. The conductor went on. Longarm pulled out a cheroot, nipped the twist off with his teeth, and cupped his hands around a match to get the smoke lighted. He was less than halfway through the cheroot when the conductor returned. The man held a wine bottle that he tucked under his arm while he brought out a fistful of bills along with a pair of quarters and two dimes.

Longarm accepted the money first, then took the wine bottle. "Thanks. I appreciate your help."

"Glad to be of service, Deputy." The conductor touched the brim of his cap and went on about his affairs.

Longarm leaned on the rail and continued to look at the vast sea of grass that was America's Great Plains. He finished his cheroot, then tossed it onto the rail bed beneath the moving car.

He made his way back through the train for half a dozen more cars before he reached the door to the baggage car.

The door was locked, bolted from the other side.

It should not be.

Passengers were permitted access to their goods while aboard. There were no connecting doors into freight or cattle cars, but baggage cars were supposed to be open.

Longarm frowned.

The baggage handler back in Denver had been most unwelcoming, and it appeared that Longarm had been right to be suspicious.

Something was up, and whatever it was, it was on the other side of this door.

Chapter 6

The railroad likely would not appreciate someone breaking down their door, and the clatter and clack of steel wheels rumbling over iron rails was much too loud for eavesdropping. But there was an alternative.

Longarm set his wine bottle full of water for the cat onto the floor of the platform, where it promptly fell over and rolled off onto the bed of gravel rushing past underneath the car.

Longarm rotated his shoulders and swung his arms to loosen his muscles, then reached for a rung of the steel ladder bolted to the end wall of the car. It took only moments to clamber up the rungs to the top of the moving car.

He climbed onto the catwalk that ran along the roof of the car and scrambled on hands and knees to the center. It would have been easier—and gentler on his trousers—to simply stand up and cover the distance upright, but the sound of his boots striking wood would very probably have been heard below and a nagging sense that something was wrong down there made him prefer silence over comfort.

He located the side door by peering over the edge, then

carefully lowered himself over the side and onto the steel ladder there. The sliding cargo door was open to the air, which made things easier for him, but even if it had been closed he could have just slid it open. Probably. As it was, he was able to take a step to the side and gain the doorway opening. He transferred one hand from the ladder to the doorjamb and pulled himself into the opening.

"Why, gentlemen, what do we have here?"

There were three of them inside the baggage car, the freight agent who had been so unpleasant back in Denver and two seedy-looking pieces of shit who were helping the son of a bitch rifle through the baggage. Likely they were a pair of brakemen working in cahoots with the agent.

At the moment Longarm joined them, the two chums were busily removing valuables from the bags while the freight agent held a large bag to receive all the goodies, like a kid begging for candy on All Hallow's Eve.

Longarm noticed his own carpetbag sitting open on the pile of bags already robbed. Not that he carried so much that might attract a thief. Unless they wanted his clean balbriggans.

"Look, I, uh, I can explain this. We heard, um, we heard there was some contraband in one of these bags. We're just trying to find it," the freight agent stammered.

Longarm smiled at the man. "An' I believe you, friend. Yeah. I really do."

"We, um, we wasn't doing nothing wrong."

"Freddy," one of the brakemen said, "this man don't believe you, not a word of it." The man—he was a scrawny fellow with unkempt black hair and three days' growth of beard—reached deep into a pocket of his coveralls and produced a small, nickel-plated popgun. It looked to Longarm like a Smith & Wesson top-break .32. Picayune but certainly large enough to kill a fellow.

"You got two choices, mister. Jump out that door and take your chances when you hit the ground, or stand there and I shoot you."

Longarm suspected the brakeman had not noticed the Colt that rode just under the open edge of his tweed coat. Either that or the idiot had a death wish.

"The train is moving too fast and that's gravel down there, not soft earth. I'd be hurt bad if I jumped, maybe even killed," Longarm said. He was willing to reason with the asshole. "Don't you think there's another possibility?"

"Mister, I gave you all the choices you're gonna get." The brakeman gave Longarm what he probably thought was a menacing scowl and ostentatiously cocked his pip-squeak revolver.

"You ain't very bright, are you?" Longarm asked calmly. "Now put that thing away before I have t'hurt you."

The brakeman pointed the .32 at Longarm.

Longarm pointed a .45 at the brakeman, pulling it in a flash from beneath his coat.

"Oh, shit," the brakeman moaned.

"Exactly," Longarm agreed.

"Shoot him, Howard, shoot him," the second brakeman shouted.

Howard obligingly shoved the muzzle of his .32 toward Longarm, presumably readying himself to kill.

He did not have time. Longarm's bullet ripped his throat out, sending a gout of blood spraying warm and sticky over the other brakeman. The freight agent, Freddy, took one look at the blood, bent over, and puked into his bag of loot.

Lordy, Longarm thought, I hope there's nothing of mine in that bag.

Chapter 7

This whole thing was a pain in the ass, Longarm thought.
Thanks to Howard and Freddy and the third man, whose
name was Andrew, Longarm would have to waste his time
getting the dead one's corpse tended to and the live ones
put behind bars.

The only alternative would be to pitch the dead man out
onto the tracks and let the live ones go. He did not think
Billy Vail would approve, so he cuffed Freddy and Andrew
to a ladder rung on the platform at the front of the baggage
car and left them there while he went up the train to find the
conductor.

"Something else I can do for you, Deputy?"

"Uh-huh. I'm gonna have to get off at Sterling with some
prisoners. Have to take my cat cage off too, I'm afraid, as
this is gonna take some time when I get on the ground."

The conductor nodded. "Whatever you need, Deputy.
You can see Freddy about helping you with that cage."

"Sorry to tell you, but Freddy is one o' the prisoners I
mentioned."

"Freddy? Why . . . what . . . ?"

Longarm gave the man a brief explanation of what had been going on in the baggage car, which elicited a loud "son of a *bitch*!"

"We've had some complaints about lost or stolen items, but I had no idea. The line had no idea. Oh, this is terrible."

"Yeah, it's terrible, but if it makes you feel any the better, they been caught now. It's over an' done with."

"Thank goodness. Yes, take whatever time you need in Sterling. I can hold the train for you if you need more time than our normal stop."

"Thanks. I'll let you know."

Longarm went back through the rumbling cars. Freddy and Andrew were unhappily waiting where he had left them.

"You boys can look forward to a long rest at the state's expense. I'll see you get comfortable accommodations down in Canon City."

"We were just, you know, pilfering a few things. We weren't really doing any harm," Andrew said.

"Could be the judge will see it that way. Most likely, though, he won't take it light. Not when you'll be charged with the attempted murder of a federal peace officer in addition to grand theft. Maybe some other stuff too."

"We didn't mean . . ."

Longarm turned his back on them and went to stand inside the car immediately ahead of the baggage car. He was protected there from the rain that was beginning to fall.

Freddy and Andrew were soon soaked through. They did not look happy.

Chapter 8

Sterling was a village with some grand pretensions about itself. For one thing it had a chief of police instead of the usual town marshal. Not that that made a lick of difference to Longarm. Their police chief was a nice young fellow named Boyd Underwood. He was quick to offer Longarm any assistance he could render.

"Couple things," Longarm told him, looking out into what had turned into a booming thunderstorm accompanied by a frog strangler of a downpour. "I could use some help getting my stuff off that baggage car. I can handle the prisoners by m'self of course. You got a jail I can stash them in?"

"Yes, of course. Right down the block there. It's the place with the big sign out front that reads 'City Jail,' " Underwood said.

"Ah, yes. That would be a clue." Longarm chuckled, and the police chief looked mildly relieved to see that his little joke had not given offense.

"I got a bag. I retrieved it once the thieves had got done with it. Put it atop my cage. That has to come off the car

too, I expect. Time I get through here, the train will be halfway to Julesburg."

"Cage?"

"I'm, well, I'm traveling with a cat. Big black sonu-
vabitch."

"A cat?"

"That's right."

"That would be one of those attack cats you federal people have been using lately?"

"Read about them, have you? This one of mine, I'm tellin' you he has to be the smartest cat in captivity. When I
first got him, I could get away with spelling stuff I didn't
want Sam to understand. That only lasted a little while.
Now that he's learned to spell, it's hard to get anything past
him. I'm trying semaphore, but I'm not sure how long it'll
be before he figures that out too."

Underwood nodded like he believed every word of it.
Then he turned serious and said, "I'll go round up some
men to fetch your things. I don't want to hold the train up
any longer than need be."

"While you're doing that, Chief, I'll bring those prisoners down to your jail. I'll meet you there."

"Call me Boyd, Deputy. I'm not much for formalities."

"An' I'm Longarm." Longarm offered his hand and the
two men shook.

Longarm ducked into a nearby mercantile, took a slicker
off a rack of them being offered for sale, and called back to
the proprietor. "I'm gonna borrow this for a few minutes."
He was out the door with the slicker draped over his head
and shoulders before the surprised man behind the store
counter could react.

Longarm climbed onto the train, paused to let the conductor know what was going on, then found his way back
to the baggage car again. He dipped two fingers into the

watch pocket sewn into the waistband of his trousers and produced the key to unlock the handcuffs that held Freddy and Andrew out there in the teeth of the storm.

"I'm gonna put these bracelets back into my coat pocket. That leaves you fellas free to walk over to the jail with me. If you feel like making a run for it, you're welcome to try. If you can outrun a .45 slug you'll make it too."

Neither prisoner said anything. They did not look like happy men with their hair plastered tight to their skulls and rainwater streaming down their faces.

By the time Longarm herded Freddy and Andrew to the next car forward, where there were some steps for them to descend—it would not do to allow a prisoner to have an accident jumping off the train—there were three men back at the baggage car removing the cage. Sam was anything but happy when the rain hit him. Longarm could hear the spitting and yowling from two cars away.

Both prisoners broke into a run as soon as their feet hit the ground, but Longarm did not get excited. Didn't shoot them either. They were only trying to run out of the rain. As soon as they reached the porch overhang in front of the mercantile where Longarm had borrowed the slicker, they stopped.

"Wait here a second," Longarm told them. He went inside and returned the dripping slicker to its place on the sales rack. "Thanks," he called to a still confused storekeeper.

"All right," he said when he was back on the boardwalk. "The jail is down that way."

Underwood was already there. He shepherded Longarm's prisoners into a patented iron cell, a prefabricated pair of units sold by Dan Johnson & Son, Lexington, Kentucky, the very latest in jail equipment.

"Do you want to keep the key?" he offered once both were secured inside one of the cells.

"No need for that. I expect I'll be gone long before they will. Unless you'd like to hang them tonight and save a lot of bother." He thought he could see both Freddy and Andrew turning pale behind those bars.

"We'll talk about it over supper, if you'd like to be my guest," Underwood offered. "We can eat at the same hotel where I had your, um, things taken. I took that liberty because you're pretty certain to be here overnight. There won't be another train until tomorrow, and the one you came on is pulling out right now."

"Yeah, I noticed," Longarm said.

"Will a hotel dinner be all right by you? I'd invite you to have a home-cooked meal at my house except for two things. I'm not married. And I don't know how to cook."

"I've always fancied hotel cooking anyway."

"This way," Underwood said, leading the way outside. Over his shoulder he called back, "You boys be good in there now. If you need anything, ring for maid service."

"You do run a fine jail, Boyd."

"I do, don't I?" Underwood agreed with a smile.

Chapter 9

The Doane House was a small affair with six rooms and a dining room. In larger communities it would have been considered a boardinghouse. Here it was the biggest building in town.

The place was run by a widow who probably was a consumptive, judging by her constant cough and her scrawny frame. If the woman had two ounces of extra weight on her, Longarm did not know where she hid it. Her dress looked like it had been made for someone two sizes bigger than Helena Doane. But then probably she was two sizes larger when she had it made.

"Hello, Boyd. It's nice to see you today. Is this the gentleman with that handsome cat?"

"The very one, Helena." Underwood made the introductions.

Mrs. Doane looked Longarm over like she was judging a horse at auction. For a moment he thought she was going to reach out and feel his biceps. "It is very nice to meet you, Mr. Long."

"Thank you, ma'am. Likewise."

"Chicken and dumplings for dinner today, Boyd."

"You do know how to get to a boy's heart."

"I know it's your favorite." She turned her attention—she had huge eyes, very bright; violet, Longarm thought; striking—to Longarm and asked, "What about you, Mr. Long? Or should I cook something special for you?"

"Chicken and dumplin's suits me fine, ma'am."

"Call me Helena."

"Yes, ma'am." The woman was a good ten or fifteen years older than Longarm. "Ma'am" seemed appropriate to him. Calling her by her given name would not have felt right.

"You know the way, Boyd. Go ahead on in. I'll tell Nellie you are here."

Mrs. Doane went off toward the back of the hotel while Underwood led the way into the empty dining room. The place held eight tables, each with four chairs. Underwood and Longarm were the only patrons in it.

Before they had time to get properly settled, a slim black girl came scurrying out of the kitchen carrying a coffeepot and a basket of freshly baked yeast rolls. The girl—she could not have been more than seventeen—kept her head down. Shy, Longarm thought. She kept glancing back toward the kitchen door.

"I don't see her," Underwood whispered. "It's all right." The young police chief startled Longarm by lifting his face to Nellie's and giving her a tender kiss.

"Please be careful," she said in a very soft voice.

"Sorry," he whispered. "Tonight?"

Nellie bit her lip, hesitated for a moment, then nodded. She gathered her skirts and almost ran back into the kitchen.

Underwood peered closely at Longarm, then said, "You don't look offended."

"Should I be?"

"Most would be."

"Maybe you're worrying before you need to," Longarm suggested.

"I love her," Underwood confessed. "We'd get married except the law says we can't. Miscegenation is what the law calls it. Bullshit is what I call that. It's perfectly all right for me to sleep with her. I can even have kids by her. But I'm not allowed to marry her. It's driving us both crazy."

"Do you live together?" Longarm asked.

Underwood shook his head.

"Maybe you should. Move her in with you. I'd bet about half the folks wouldn't give a shit. And *you* shouldn't give a shit about the ones who'd disapprove. It ain't any o' their business."

"Most of the town council are old fuddy-duddies. First thing would be that I'd lose my job."

Longarm took a sip of the coffee Nellie had poured for him. It was hot and fresh and very good. "That's different," he said.

Underwood sighed. "So we sneak around and are miserable."

"Would you be more miserable without her?"

"Yeah. I sure would."

"Mind a suggestion from a total stranger?"

"Longarm, I'd welcome a suggestion from old Lucifer if it would let me be with Nellie more than this."

Longarm leaned back in his chair. "Get you a list of official post offices in all the states. I seen such a book once. It's real complete. Then find an atlas an' look up all the little towns in, oh, Vermont, Maine, places like that. Write to the town councils in each of 'em and ask do they need a chief of police, which is what you already are here. Say you're wanting a change for yourself and your wife. Find you a job back

East, then jump over the broomstick with her an' the two of
you get on an eastbound train. Might take some time an' a
whole lot o' letter writing, but I bet it could be done."

"Jump over a broomstick?" Underwood asked.

Longarm laughed. "Nellie will know what it means. It's
what the slaves did to 'marry' each other when their owners
wouldn't allow real wedding ceremonies. It's a commitment 'tween man and wife. Which is what a marriage is anyway. A down-deep commitment. Then if sometime you can
find a preacher who'll do the job proper, well, you can have
that too. Meantime just take the girl an' go."

"Interesting thought," Underwood said. "I'll talk it over
with Nellie tonight."

"You two lovebirds do that," Longarm said. "In the meantime let's us have some of that chicken an' dumplin's. I can
smell it from here an' it has my mouth to waterin'." He
shook out his napkin and tucked it under his chin.

Nellie appeared again, this time carrying a large tureen
and pair of bowls.

Chapter 10

Longarm spent the afternoon writing his report about the
thefts and the shooting. He had to write it out three times,
as there was neither a typewriting machine nor an amanu-
ensis in the town—one copy for Billy Vail, one copy for the
railroad, and another copy for Chief Underwood.

He did not know where or before what judge Freddy and
Andrew would be tried. That would be hashed out between
the railroad and Underwood. A flurry of telegraph messages
between the railroad's local manager, a surly, aging man
named William Watson, and their Denver offices claimed
the pair should be returned to Denver for trial. Boyd Underwood wanted to keep them for trial before the town magis-
trate.

Longarm could not see that it made much difference. Either way they would wind up serving prison sentences in
Canon City, and probably the length of the sentences would
be much the same no matter which court they were tried in.

"Boyd," Longarm said late in the afternoon, "are you a
drinkin' man?"

"I'm not one for getting drunk if that's what you mean, but I've been known to take a drink now and then."

Longarm leaned back in the police chief's swivel chair, which he had borrowed while he studiously wrote those cursed reports. He stretched and yawned and said, "I'm buyin'. If you're interested, that is."

"I could stand a drink."

"Lead the way then." He stood and stretched again, then extended his fingers, made a fist, and opened his hand wide once more, flexing his fingers in and out repeatedly. After all that time with the shaft of an ink pen in hand, his hand was cramped and aching.

Longarm grabbed his Stetson off a rack by the door and followed Underwood out into the waning sunlight. They walked to a small saloon at the edge of town.

The place was not fancy but it was nice. Built long and narrow, the bar extended along the left side wall while a few very small tables were placed here and there in the remaining space. Patrons were expected to stand at the bar. If they wanted to rest, they could prop their feet on the brass rail that ran along the front of the bar.

The backbar was lined with bottles, and the beer mugs were made of glass, both a good sign that it was likely to be a calm and quiet environment where a man could drink without worrying about some son of a bitch throwing a chair at him.

There were five other men propped up along the bar when Longarm and Boyd came in. The proprietor, who served as his own barman, was out in front of his bar lighting the oil lamps that were suspended from the ceiling on two racks. The back set of lamps was already burning. The man waved a brief greeting, finished lighting the last of the four lamps on the forward rack, and pulled the thin chain to draw the rack up toward the ceiling. Once he had secured the lamp chain, he returned to his place behind the bar.

"Hello, Boyd." He nodded a greeting to Longarm and asked, "Your usual, Boyd? And what about you, mister?"

"The usual," Underwood agreed. "Tom, this is Deputy United States Marshal Custis Long."

"Of course. You're the gentleman who brought in those thieves off the train and shot that brakeman." Tom smiled and extended his hand to shake. "What will you have, Deputy? The first one is on me as a thank-you for making our town safer. Anyone who would steal like that would do other things too. We don't need that sort around." The saloonkeeper pushed a wooden bowl of peanuts closer to hand for them.

"Thank you, Tom. Reckon I'll take you up on that offer an' have me a whiskey. Rye if you have it."

"Indeed I do. Best quality too." He poured a beer for Boyd Underwood and for Longarm selected a slightly dusty bottle from his array of choices. He poured with a generous hand and set the tumbler in front of Longarm. "Tell me what you think of that."

Longarm smelled the whiskey, took a tentative sip, then broke into a broad grin. "Now, that, sir, is the real deal. Maryland?"

"Nothing but," Tom agreed.

"You've made a long day worthwhile." This was whiskey to savor slowly rather than toss back.

"Glad I could help, Deputy." Tom left the two of them and went back along the length of his bar to see how he could accommodate his other customers.

"Nice fellow," Longarm observed.

"That thing we were talking about earlier," Underwood said.

"What thing?"

"Writing those letters." He glanced down the bar to make sure Tom was not close and lowered his voice. "Looking for a job back East. Would you, um, would you give me a recommendation? It might help if I could say I had the endorsement of a deputy marshal with your reputation."

"How would you work that, Boyd? I can't sit down an' write out a hundred or so notes of recommendation."

"I thought about that, Longarm. If you agree, I could mention you and invite them to write to you at the marshal's office in Denver. Aside from meaning you wouldn't have to pen all those notes, it would assure any interested parties that the endorsement was for real."

Longarm nodded and took another small swallow of his rye. "Makes sense."

"If you are willing, that is."

"Sure. I'll stand up for you. Wish I could stand up for you in front of a marrying judge too."

Underwood smiled. "I can't wait to tell Nellie about this."

Longarm tossed back the rest of his drink. "Then let's go have supper. My treat this time. Maybe if there ain't too many diners you'll have a chance to give your lady the news."

Underwood looked like he was going to cry. "Lady," he said. "Lord God, Longarm, I've never heard another human person refer to her like that."

"Then it's damn well about time, isn't it. Come along, Boyd. I dunno about you, but I'm feeling awful hungry all of a sudden."

Chapter 11

They had a leisurely supper of beef fried in tallow, then carried their coffee cups with them out onto the porch that ran along the front of the building. The two lawmen sat in comfortable silence while the light melted out of the western sky and cicadas began to chirr. When the last cups of coffee were gone, Underwood stood.

"If you'll excuse me, Longarm, I need to make my rounds before, well, you know."

"Indeed I do." The police chief had found a moment to speak with Nellie. There was not enough time for him to tell her everything, but he'd told her enough to put the light of excitement into her brown eyes. Underwood looked as eager as a kid now.

"Give me your cup," Longarm said. "I'll take them inside."

"I'll see you in the morning," Underwood said. "Tell you everything then."

"That's a promise." Longarm took the empty cups inside. Over the sounds of clattering dishes in the back he could hear someone humming. He could guess who that might be.

He went back onto the porch and sat in a rocker while he smoked a cheroot. When he was finished with it, he stood and flicked the cigar butt into the street. He felt like he had been chained to a chair the whole damned day, and he wanted to stretch his legs to loosen up a bit before he turned in. He walked down to the rails, silent at this time of night, and east along the right-of-way for ten minutes or so, then turned and started back.

When he neared the switch shack where a train could be diverted onto a side track if need be, he heard a sound. A scraping in the gravel of the roadbed. A grunt and then another. He heard a squeal and a man's voice growled, "Little bitch bit me," followed by the sound of a slap.

Longarm rounded the switch shack to find two men struggling with a small woman. They had her skirt and underdrawers off so that she wore only a blouse and her shoes. The woman's flesh was dark, he noticed.

She was being assaulted by two men, either one of whom was twice her size.

Longarm walked up to them and tapped the nearer man on the shoulder. Judging from his reaction, he was a jumpy sort. He damned near came out of his skin when Longarm touched him.

"Excuse me for interrupting," Longarm said, his tone mild and pleasant, "but it don't look to me like the lady wants you boys to do whatever it is you're tryin' to do."

"Butt out, mister."

"No, sir, I expect I can't do that. Not unless the lady tells me to go."

"I said butt out. And don't be calling this little slut no lady. She's not but a nigger bitch."

"Mr. Long, is that you, sir?" the girl asked. She sounded upset. Rather understandably so.

"Yes, it is. Is that you, Nellie?"

"Yes, sir." She shook the larger man's hand off her shoulder and stood upright. "Yes, sir."

Longarm turned slightly away from her as she struggled back into her clothes. "What were these men doing, Nellie?" he asked.

"You know what they were doing, Mr. Long, sir."

"I need to hear you say it, Nellie."

"They was trying to rape me, sir." She drew in a deep, shuddering breath. "They done that before, sir." She began to cry. "They done it before."

"Well, boys," Longarm said cheerfully, "you just hit the jackpot. You've committed rape and attempted rape. Between 'em, I expect you'll be spending ten to twelve in Canon City."

"Rape, hell," one of the men retorted. "She's just a nigger. That ain't rape."

"It's just what you call an amusement," the other one said.

"You call it one thing, I call it another. The opinion that matters is what a judge calls it."

Longarm heard a chuckle. "Hell, take us in if you like then. Tomorrow morning Judge Loomis will get a good laugh out of this and we'll be right back out again."

"Thanks for the warning," Longarm said. "In that case I'd best send you down the line to Denver for trial there. You won't find any favoritism there, boys."

"Hey, you can't do that," one of them bawled.

"Sure I can. I'm a federal peace officer. Just watch me an' see."

"I am *not* going to prison for having me a little dark meat."

"Then you'd best get you one hellacious fine lawyer because I can personally testify as to what I seen here."

"You can testify? Not if you're dead, you son of a bitch."
The man's hand went to his waist and Longarm saw the
gleam of moonlight on steel.

He reacted without taking time for conscious thought.
His big Colt filled his hand, and before the rapist could
shoot, Longarm squeezed off two quick shots. The muzzle
flash lighted up the night for a dozen yards around and the
man fell back with two .45 slugs in his chest.

Longarm shifted his attention to the other man. "Are you
taking a hand in this?"

"N-n-no, sir, I ain't, I'm not . . . Oh, Jesus! Henry? Henry?"

Henry gurgled a little, rolled onto his side, and died, his
body deflating like an empty husk.

"Nellie, are you afraid to stay here alone with a corpse
until I can get Boyd over here?"

"No, sir, Mr. Long. You go ahead. I'll be all right."

"I'll send Boyd quick as I can find him."

Longarm took his prisoner to the jail and locked him
into the cell adjacent to Freddy and Andrew's. Then Longarm met Underwood on the street as he was coming out of
the jail.

"Was that you I heard shooting, Longarm?"

"Yeah, so it was." Longarm filled the local police chief
in on what happened and said, "I took the liberty of putting
the bastard in your jail."

"I wish you'd shot him too. Are you sure the other one is
dead?"

"I've seen my fair share o' dead ones, Boyd. This one
was dead sure enough. What was your girl doing out there
anyway?"

"That shack is where we've been meeting, Longarm. It's
always empty at night and there's no one around. They
never lock it, so. . . ." Underwood shrugged. "You know
how it is."

"Right. I'm sorry it had to happen to her."

"I'm just glad you were there to stop them."

As soon as Nellie caught sight of Boyd, she came running into his arms. He clung to her, rocking her back and forth and soothing her as if she were a child. "I'll, uh, write out an' sign a report on this first thing in the morning," Longarm said. He did not know if either of the lovebirds heard him. He turned and started back toward town and the saloon, where he could find another drink of that good rye whiskey.

Chapter 12

It was late when Longarm finally made it back to the hotel. Helena Doane met him at the door. She looked disapproving, which he assumed was because he was keeping her waiting for him so she could lock up. Instead she snapped, "You would have kept that poor, dear thing hungry and uncared for. Lucky for you I took care of him."

"Him? No offense but . . . who the hell are you talkin' about?"

"That lovely cat, of course. He needed food and grooming. I took care of that. Cleaned his sandbox and gave that beautiful coat a good brushing. I swear, I do not know why you would go to the bother of traveling with him if you'll not take proper care of him."

"Ma'am, I'm travelin' with that albatross only 'cause I promised a favor to my boss. If it was left to me, I'd turn the miserable thing loose in a barn where he could catch some mice an' do somebody some good."

"You are a cruel and heartless man, Deputy Long."

"Yes, ma'am, I expect you are right on both counts. That exact same thing has been told to me on many an occasion." He touched the brim of his Stetson and said, "So if you'll excuse me, ma'am, I'd like to go up to bed now."

Mrs. Doane coughed into her hand, which Longarm took as consent. After all, she did bob her head when she coughed. Sort of.

He went up the stairs, took one of the thin, wax tapers from the box of them on a shelf, and lighted it from the oil lamp that was left burning on a small chest below the box of candles. He carried the candle into his room and used it to light the lamp at his bedside, then blew the candle out.

Sam was peering at him through the wire bars of his cage, his eyes seeming big as saucers in the dim light. The animal hissed and got his back up when Longarm leaned down to take a look at him. Mrs. Doane, he thought, must be a remarkably brave woman to risk life and limb by approaching a nasty beast like that.

No matter. Another day or two and it would be someone else's problem.

He stripped off his clothes, folding them on the chair placed by the room's window. When he was down to bare skin, he climbed in between the sheets, leaned over, and blew out the lamp flame, plunging the room into darkness.

He fell almost instantly asleep.

Chapter 13

"What? Who?" Longarm came awake even quicker than he had gone to sleep. His Colt was already in hand as he sat bolt upright on the lumpy bed in Mrs. Doane's hotel room.

He was sure . . . Yeah, there was a sliver of light at the edge of the room door, light coming from the lamp in the hall, that would be. But what . . . ?

He heard the creak of floorboards and rapid, shallow breathing.

Then he heard a subdued cough and recognized who was in the room. Was that her deal then? Entice guests to her hotel and rob them? That would seem like a piss-poor plan considering that as far as he knew there was no one else staying in the tiny hotel. The list of suspects would be almighty short if a robbery was reported.

And she did know that he was a deputy United States marshal. Boyd Underwood had introduced him as such.

If the woman was not here to rob him, then what the devil was she doing in his room? Surely she couldn't have sneaked in just to mess with the damned cat. With a sub-

dued sigh, he dropped the revolver back into the holster he
had placed near the head of the bed.

The answer to his questions about what she wanted in
his room was not long in coming. He felt the edge of the
bed tilt, and a warm, skin-and-bones body slipped beneath
the thin sheet that covered him.

A hand, surprisingly gentle, found his cock, stroking and
coaxing it into an erection. Not that it took so very much
coaxing. He came to life and heard a gasp—he thought a
pleased one—as Helena Doane discovered how damned big
Custis Long was in the parts that count.

She bent over him and began kissing and licking his
chest, starting just below his throat and working her way
down his body.

Longarm tried to give a little in return by stroking and
petting her. His roaming hands found prominent ribs covered by tight, stretched skin and hard nipples where tits
should have been. The woman had less meat on her than a
skeleton twice picked over by buzzards.

Her mouth, however, was warm and moist. Hell, it was
hot and wet.

Her tongue probed into his belly button while she fon-
dled his balls with one hand.

That hand moved up onto the shaft of his now very interested cock. She steadied his dick and peeled his foreskin
back, then ran the tip of her tongue around and around the
head. She kept that up until Longarm was beginning to think
that was all she intended to do.

By way of persuasion, he reached down and nudged the
back of her head, pressing her down onto his pecker.

Mrs. Doane took the hint. She opened wide and took
him deep into her mouth. She gagged when the head of his
cock reached the entrance to her throat. She backed off and
tried again with the same result. The third time was the

charm, and his cock slid past the ring of cartilage there and he was socketed completely inside her mouth and throat.

She started to gag again and quickly withdrew, but continued to bob her head up and down, taking the head of his prick into the warmth of her mouth and out again.

As Longarm's breathing quickened, so did the rapidity and strength of her sucking. All too quickly—dammit he was not ready to stop those marvelous sensations yet—he felt the rise of pressure in his balls and then the sweet explosion of cum driving up through his shaft and into Helena's mouth.

He relaxed with a sigh and idly rolled her nipple between his thumb and forefinger.

He pulled her up beside him on the narrow bed, put a hand between her thighs—they felt about as big around as pipe stems—and slowly fingered her. She was already wet and ready to receive him.

His hard-on swelled full again. She tried to tug him on top of her, but the truth was that Longarm was afraid he would break something inside her if he gave his weight to her. Instead he rolled her onto her belly, knelt behind her, and took her dog style.

Mrs. Doane cried out—in pleasure, he hoped—when he entered her pussy. She rocked back against him, then kept it up with each forward stroke he took.

The blow job she gave him had taken the edge off so that he had much longer staying power once he was inside her. He held onto her hips. They were mostly bone covered by a thin sheaf of skin. At least that gave him a good handhold. He increased the speed and the strength of his thrusts until he was pounding her ass, his swinging balls slapping against her with each plunge.

Helena began to whimper. She shook her head wildly back and forth and began to shudder.

All of a sudden she screamed. Startled the hell out of Longarm when she did it. Then she went limp, falling face-forward onto the bed.

She pulled free of his dick when she dropped, leaving him chilling in the cool night air.

Then she began to snore.

What the hell, he thought. He wedged himself in between Mrs. Doane and the bedroom wall. He closed his eyes and once again he was asleep within moments.

Chapter 14

Longarm dimly remembered Mrs. Doane leaving his bed sometime during the night. When he got up the next morning, he was alone. He poured a little water into the basin placed on a small table, dipped the accompanying washcloth into the water, and washed off some of the sticky residues left over from his nighttime frolic.

He dressed quickly, then raised the roller blind to get a look outside. Yesterday's rain had cleared. Now the sky was deep blue in the early morning light.

When he went downstairs, he was greeted as if he were a total stranger, just another overnight guest in the hotel. "Breakfast in fifteen minutes, Mr. Long."

"Yes, ma'am." He went out onto the front porch and sat in a rocking chair to have a morning smoke. The timing worked out well. At the same moment his cheroot was done, the promised breakfast was ready.

The woman could cook; he had to give her that much. Truth be told she could also fuck like a mink and suck well enough to pull a .45 slug through a .22-caliber barrel.

Longarm was just finishing his meal when Boyd Underwood showed up.

"Looks like I missed you," Underwood said. "I take it you're leaving?"

"No, I'll set an' have another cup o' coffee while you eat."

Underwood eyed the grease that was left on Longarm's empty plate. "What's for breakfast this morning?"

"Chops o' some kind. Lamb, I think. And fried taters."

Underwood grinned. "Miz Doane likes you, Longarm."

"How can you tell that when she isn't even in the room for you to see?"

The grin got wider. "Guests she doesn't like get oat porridge, and if she *really* doesn't like them the porridge is scorched."

Longarm laughed.

"Boyd, what lies have you been telling this gentleman?" Mrs. Doane asked from the kitchen doorway.

"Nothing but the truth, ma'am."

Mrs. Doane returned to her kitchen, and moments later Nellie entered the dining room carrying Boyd's breakfast. It was the same as Longarm's had been. Apparently the woman liked him too. And Nellie most certainly did.

"Did you two have a chance to talk after I left you last night?" Longarm whispered when both women had gone back into the kitchen.

Underwood nodded. "She's excited about the idea. Now I can't imagine why we didn't think of this before. I'll get started on those letters first thing. I already checked on my way over here. Our post office has a copy of that book you mentioned. The postmaster said I can borrow it for as long as I like. I, uh, didn't tell him why I want it, of course."

"I have to come over and get that shooting report made out this morning. Remind me to write down the marshal's business address so's you can get that recommendation whenever you need. Oh, and I'll need your help rounding up a luggage cart and a couple husky youngsters to haul the damned cat over to the depot for me."

"You haven't shot the thing yet?"

"Thought about it, but it turns out Miz Doane is one of those women that's crazy about cats. She's already been upstairs to feed the damn thing an' do whatever else it is that a cat needs."

"We'll go over to my office soon as I finish my breakfast. On the way over I'll get those boys for you. Mrs. Doane can show them upstairs to fetch the cage."

"Miserable damn thing," Longarm grumbled.

"Quit your bitching and let's get to work. There ought to be just about time enough to get your report written out before the Julesburg train pulls in."

Chapter 15

Longarm—and cat—arrived in Julesburg on time, only to
find there was a layover before the connecting eastbound
would pull in. Longarm paid a kid ten cents to babysit the
miserable beast while he went to get a bite to eat. When he
got back, he produced the promised dime and said, "Okay,
son, I'll take over now."

"I'll sit beside a cage anytime for ten whole cents, mister. Thanks." The boy gave him a parting grin and ran scam-
pering away, probably to brag to his buddies about the easy
mark sitting at the Union Pacific depot.

Longarm sighed and settled down on a bench where he
could keep an eye on the cage. It was put on a baggage cart
to get it off the upbound from Denver and he saw no reason
to take it off just to have to put it back on again. He picked
up a local newspaper that someone had discarded and began to read about things and people that were of absolutely
no interest to him.

"Well now, will ya lookee here." The speaker sounded
about half-drunk.

Longarm looked. So, apparently, did the two bleary-eyed

and wobbly men who were with the drunk who had spoken. The three were standing beside Sam's cage, staring at the black cat.

"I know where's we can get us some coal oil," the fellow said. He was a large, rough-looking man wearing overalls and flannel long johns but no shirt. Some sort of roustabout, Longarm guessed. His companions were dressed approximately the same. None of them seemed much interested in sartorial excellence.

"I got matches," another offered.

"Just don't let it scratch you when you open that cage. Fucker looks mean."

"It is mean," Longarm offered. "An' I have to tell you, if you intend to light that cat's tail an' turn it loose you're gonna be awful surprised."

"Why's that, mister?"

Longarm smiled, his voice and expression gentle and kind. "Because if you try it, I will naturally stomp your asses into the dirt, that's why."

The first man gave him a frankly disbelieving look. "Against the three of us?" He did not sound so drunk now for some reason. But then likely he was getting his blood up ready for a fight, and a good scrap tends to leach the alcohol from a man's system.

Longarm nodded. "Against the three of you," he affirmed.

"That's 'cause you got a gun and we don't," the third man said.

"If you insist on trying me, I'll take the gun off an' still whup your asses, guaran-damn-teed."

"Bullshit," the first fellow said. He did seem a belligerent sort. It probably would be sensible to take that one down first, Longarm thought.

"Guaranteed I said, an' guaranteed I meant."

"This we got to see." With that, all three abandoned their

interest in the cat and the cage and came charging across the U.P. platform with their fists clenched and arms flailing.

Longarm came off his bench, stepped sideways to present himself in front of the first man who'd spoken, and delivered an anvil-hard fist onto the fellow's nose. The blow snapped the man's head back and broke his nose. Blood sprayed wildly. The sight of his own blood did not slow the man in the least.

Longarm slid sideways in the other direction, and the other two came bulling completely past him. The one in the lead ran headlong into the railroad bench. Which, as it turned out, was bolted firmly in position. The man cried out and dropped onto the bench clutching his knees.

With luck, Longarm thought, the son of a bitch broke a kneecap. Maybe worse. If so . . . good.

The first man kept coming in, so Longarm poked him another time on his already broken nose, just to get his attention, then pivoted and slugged the third man, burying his fist damn near to the elbow in the fellow's gut. The man spun around, doubled over, and puked all down the front of his overalls.

Bullyboy number one tried again. Lordy but he just did not want to quit. He stepped in close, threw a punch overtop of Longarm's guard, and landed a solid blow high on Longarm's cheekbone. Half of Longarm's face went numb, but down on his neck he could feel blood beginning to flow.

"Shit, but you can punch," Longarm mumbled.

"You ain't so bad your own self." The fellow stepped back, winded, and gulped for air. "Had enough?" he asked.

"Not hardly."

The man straightened up, stepped in, and tried a feint with his left, then lashed out hard with his right. Longarm blocked it, only to feel the left sink into his belly. He grinned. "Didn't see that coming," he laughed.

"How's about this one?" The man threw another right. This time Longarm stepped in close and threw an underhand punch into the solar plexus. The fellow doubled over, gasping for air again. When he straightened again, he peered down at his fallen warriors and shook his head. "Those boys ain't near as good at fighting as they think they are."

"What about you?" Longarm asked. He pulled a bandana from his back pocket and used it to mop at the blood on his neck.

"This is fun, but I don't think I'm gonna be able to whip you. Want to get a drink instead?"

"I'd like to, but I got to keep an eye on the cat." He grinned again. "Protect the son of a bitch from people like you."

"Tell you what, Jake here an' Conrad can watch the damn cat. You and me will go over and dip our beaks in some suds. How's that sound?"

"I could stand it." Longarm extended his hand. "My name is Custis."

"I'm Leroy."

"I don't know that it's exactly a pleasure meeting you, Leroy, but what the hell." The two shook hands, and Leroy got his companions upright and paying attention.

"Jake, you guard that cat. Conrad, you'd best go clean yourself off. I hate to say this, but you stink."

Conrad was walking like a kid that has pissed himself, kind of bowlegged and trying not to let the wet cloth touch skin.

"Where're you going?" Jake asked.

"Me an' Custis here are gonna get a drink. Maybe we'll fight some more later."

Jake shrugged and went to sit closer to the cat cage.

"Come along," Leroy said. "I know just the place."

Chapter 16

Longarm was feeling mellow when the train pulled out for Omaha and points east. He did not even bother going up to the smoking car, just found a soft carpetbag—someone else's in this case—to sit on and dozed through the afternoon. Back on his original schedule although a day delayed, he arrived in Grand Island late in the evening.

The depot was deserted save for a handful of people there to meet the train or to board it. Practically within seconds those folks cleared out and went on their way, leaving Longarm virtually alone on the platform. He yawned and lighted a cheroot—really should stock up on those before he left the U.P. line, he reminded himself—then went in search of someone to help him pull the damned cat cage off the train.

It was amazing, he thought, how quickly people could disperse. Not that there had been so very many hanging around at this time of night, but now there were none.

He looked around the outside of the depot, but the usual collection of bummers and hangers-on were absent. There was a light on inside the station, so he tried in there.

"Help you, mister?" the night duty agent asked.

"I'm looking for somebody to help me pull some awkward baggage off the car," Longarm told the man.

The fellow, a fat man in sleeve garters and eyeshade, shrugged. "Sorry, mister. I'm the telegraph operator and can't leave my key. I could sell you a ticket or send a message, but that's about all."

"All right, thanks. Any idea where I might find somebody?"

"There's a saloon in the next block over. You could likely find somebody there. Have to pay them though, I would think."

"I'll try there." Longarm tapped the brim of his Stetson and hurried back out the door to round up a small work crew. After that, well, after that he was not sure when or where to find transportation on to this Wansley place where he was supposed to meet Sam's owner.

Unlike the railroad station, the saloon was doing a bang-up business despite the hour. Or perhaps because of it. A good many of the patrons appeared to be railroad men, quite possibly including the crew of the train Longarm arrived on.

A man who had a good job was not apt to be interested in the small change Longarm was willing to pay for help, so he targeted those who looked less prosperous.

"No, thanks."

"Not me, bub."

"Get the fuck outta here."

"Thank you but no."

Longarm was beginning to become a mite discouraged. Then a gent wearing a floppy engineer's cap and striped overalls that were stained with coal dust stepped close and touched his elbow to get Longarm's attention. "Yeah?"

"'Scuse me, but I overheard you asking for somebody

to help you take something off the baggage car of that east-bound?"

"That's right," Longarm said. "Are you interested?"

The fellow laughed. "Not me, mister."

"What then?"

"I guess you haven't noticed, but that train is already pulling out." He took a watch out of his pocket and checked the time. "Yep. Unless Harry is running late for some reason . . ."

But by then Longarm was no longer listening. He was racing for the door.

He got outside just in time to see the U.P. caboose glide past the station building.

Off to his right he heard a mournful hoot as the replacement engineer tugged the whistle cord.

"Shee-damn-it!" Longarm moaned. Sam and that miserable fucking cage were on their way to Omaha without him.

Chapter 17

"I'm sorry, sir, I really am, but I am not going to screw up the entire line because of your cat." The fat telegrapher did not sound particularly sorry. If anything the man's expression suggested he thought Deputy United States Marshal Custis Long was out of his mind.

"If I had the authority to send a stop order for your cat to be off-loaded, it would back up traffic across half of the country, sir. Between here and Omaha we have a very tight schedule of both freight and passenger movement. In order to stop number seventeen, that's the train carrying the cat, we would have to shunt number thirty-six onto a siding, let number four through but then put it onto a siding, and that's not even considering that it is the middle of the night and our work crews are at bare minimum. Really, sir, we just can't do it."

Longarm supposed he could have forced the issue with a display of his badge, but that would have been quite simply an abuse of power. There were no law enforcement issues about an errant cat cage.

"The best I can do, sir, is to send a message down the

line to have the cage placed in the station instead of stacked in freight storage when they pull into Omaha. Could be someone will look after it for you. I'll ask them to. And you won't be but half a day behind it."

"Yeah," Longarm growled, "but I didn't want it to go past here. I need to hire passage up to a place called Wansley. That's where I'm supposed to take the damn cat."

The night man could only shrug.

"All right, so when is the next train to Omaha?" Longarm asked.

"It's due in at 5:20 tomorrow morning." The fellow turned to look at the big Regulator clock on the wall behind him. "This morning, I should say."

Longarm tugged his Ingersoll from his vest pocket and compared it with the railroad's clock. The two timepieces were less than a minute apart. It was five minutes past midnight. Longarm had had better days than the one just past.

"Do you want a ticket to Omaha, sir?" The fellow was already reaching toward the rack of multicolored tickets covering all the destinations one could reach both east and west.

"No," Longarm said. "No, I don't."

"Whatever you say, sir."

There was no damned way Longarm was going to pay out of his own pocket for a trip to Omaha. He had no intention of paying extra for freight charges between Grand Island and Omaha either. Damn that cat anyway. And Billy Vail and Billy's wife and . . . he really was not in a very good humor at this moment.

So, 5:20 was it?

Longarm wheeled around and headed back to the saloon, but not for assistance with the cage this time. He just plain wanted a drink.

Chapter 18

Longarm yawned, scratched his belly, then rubbed his chin. This railroad travel shit was interfering with his opportunities to get a shave, and with a job to do that might not happen anytime soon either.

The conductor came through, his little blue cap bobbing with each swaying step he took as the train rocked slowly from side to side on the slightly uneven tracks.

Longarm could hear the squeal of brakes and the rustle of cloth as the train slowed and passengers stood and began to gather up their things.

"Everybody off now," the conductor called out repeatedly as he walked toward the back of the car. "End of the line, folks. Everybody off now."

Longarm waited until the train was completely stopped and the car was clearing of people before he yawned again and uncoiled himself from the seat where he had been dozing. It was 2:12 in the afternoon, three minutes ahead of the scheduled arrival in Omaha. Passengers continuing on would have to ferry across to the Council Bluffs side of the Missouri to secure transportation farther east.

Longarm walked around to the side of the station, to a door labeled "Freight." The top half of the Dutch door was open. Longarm rapped lightly on the jamb to get the freight agent's attention.

"Yes, sir?"

"You got a cat in a cage here for me?"

"And what color cat are you looking for, sir?"

"Jeez, mister, you can't tell me you have more than one damned cat in there. It's black. Not a white hair on the little bastard."

"I have a black cat, yes."

"It's still alive?"

The railroad man nodded.

"I was afraid of that," Longarm said. "Look, I'm close about to starvation, so I'm gonna go get something to eat, then pick up a prisoner I got to take back west with me. Has the cat had anything to eat?"

"Damned if I'd know. I didn't do anything with it."

"All right, thanks."

"You're not going to take it with you?"

"Lord, no. Not right now anyhow. When I get back, I'll want to ship it back west to Grand Island. That's where it was supposed to come off the other day."

"Whatever you say, mister. It won't be going anywhere."

"Thanks."

Longarm left the Union Pacific depot and walked a block and a half, until he found a decent-looking restaurant. The place served fat beef fried in tallow with mountains of fried potatoes on the side, just his kind of meal. And rhubarb pie for dessert, tart underneath a crust of baked-on cane sugar. The coffee was a little weak, but he could forgive that in light of everything else.

"Twenty-five cents," the waitress told him when he laid his napkin beside his plate.

"That cover everything?" he asked.

"It does."

She wasn't much for pretty, but the woman was just fine for efficient. He placed three dimes beside his plate and picked up his Stetson, then dipped his head and touched the brim of the hat toward her.

Omaha's city jail was a three-story affair not far from the river. These were facts Longarm had not known, but the hansom driver did. The price of the cab would come out of the marshal's budget, this being in the way of official business from here on back to Denver . . . and never mind if a detour had to be taken through Wansley.

A desk mounted high on a platform was in the lobby of the jail. Two men in blue uniform coats sat behind it.

"Help you, mister?" asked the older, a man with sergeant's stripes on his sleeve.

Longarm produced his wallet and showed his badge. "Deputy U.S. marshal," he said, "here to collect a Delbert Schrank for transport back to Denver."

"Name?"

"Schrank. Delb—"

"Your name, not his," the sergeant interrupted.

"Oh. Long," Longarm said. "Custis Long."

The man grunted and nodded his head. "Your marshal wired that you'd be coming. The reason I asked your name is because there's word on the street that this fellow's friends don't want him to testify. Fact is, there was an attempt on his life yesterday. One of our people stopped it, but your man is shaken pretty badly. I don't think he wants to testify now."

"That ain't my worry. All I have to do is get him there," Longarm said.

"Alive," the sergeant put in.

"Yes, well, there is that."

The sergeant turned to his companion. "Dave, go fetch Schrank for the gentleman."

Dave grunted and picked up a bulky ring of keys. He turned and disappeared into the jail proper.

"He won't be but a minute," the sergeant offered. "You can get started signing your life away while Dave is bringing your prisoner down."

Longarm went around to the other side of the desk and produced the written order, signed by a federal judge, that Henry had given him back in Denver. Paperwork. It was a pain in the ass, but it had to be done.

Chapter 19

"Look now," Longarm said, "I'm tired as hell an' grouchy as a bear in hibernation. I been on a train, seems like since sometime the middle o' last month. It's late in the day and I'd sure as hell like t'get some sleep before I start back. Will it be all right if I leave Schrank where he is till tomorrow morning?"

"Will you feds pay for his feed and lodging? He's already been signed over to you, you know."

Longarm shrugged. "I suppose so."

The desk sergeant shuffled through his desk drawers to produce the proper form, brought it out, and again pushed the pen and ink pot over for Longarm's use. "Just sign here to authorize the payment and we'll keep him for you. Come to that, Deputy, we'll hold the son of a bitch long as you like if your people pay for his keep."

Pay the jail fees or pay for Schrank's hotel lodging and meals, it was all the same to Longarm. He dipped the nib of the pen into the city's purple ink and signed where the sergeant indicated.

"I'll check the train schedule and be back for him in the morning," he said.

"He'll be here."

Longarm walked out into what little remained of the evening daylight. The air was becoming cool, and he wished he had brought a heavier coat instead of the thin tweed garment he preferred for city wear.

The café where he had lunch earlier had been just fine, so he went back there, only to find it already closed. Painted on the inside of the door glass were the hours of operation. The place opened only for breakfast and lunch. A family outfit, no doubt. Longarm went grumbling in search of an alternate eatery.

The restaurant he finally found was more expensive and less friendly than the little café had been. And the food was not as good either. He was in a shitty mood when he checked into a hotel close to the Union Pacific depot.

"No luggage?" the clerk asked, eyeing Longarm with obvious suspicion.

"Over at the depot," he answered.

"Sure it is. Cash up front, please."

Longarm sighed. This was not the best day he'd ever had.

Instead of laying out his own cash, he pulled a payment authorization form from his coat pocket and gave the clerk a look at that and at his badge.

"Well, all right then."

Longarm made sure the smart-ass little son of a bitch filled out the date and amount to his satisfaction before he signed the chit. Finally the man handed him a key and directions to his room upstairs.

"No women overnight," the clerk warned. "If you do, you'll have to pay extra."

Longarm was too tired to invite a woman to his room even if he'd had one nearby. Which he did not.

"Send your boy up with a bottle o' rye whiskey," he mumbled over his shoulder as he mounted the stairs. That would come out of his own pocket too, of course. Tired as he was, it would be worth it to avoid having to go out and find a saloon.

If the bellboy ever did bring a bottle upstairs to him, Longarm never knew it. He was asleep within seconds of entering the hotel room.

Chapter 20

He woke sometime before dawn. He felt . . . he felt damn good is what he felt actually. Rested. Refreshed. Ready for a new day.

Longarm stood and stretched, then crossed to the window looking out over the back alley. He pulled back the curtains and opened the window to let in the chill morning air. He breathed deep, yawned, and stretched again, loosening muscles that had become cramped on the long train ride to get here.

Off to the east, above the rooflines of the buildings facing the next street over, he could see the red and orange streaks of a new dawn. There was something sailors said about that. He could not remember all of it, but the first part, he thought, was "red sky at night, sailor's delight." A red sky in the morning was supposed to be bad if he remembered correctly. Not that he really cared if it rained today. He and Schrank would be warm and comfortable—well, more or less—inside a Union Pacific railroad coach.

Longarm took a moment just to breathe the cool, clean air of morning, then turned and went to the bedside table

where he had piled his things. He dressed quickly and pulled
on his boots, stamping his feet a few times to settle them
on his feet. That brought a complaint from someone in a
nearby room.

"Shut the fuck up!"

Direct and to the point, Longarm noted. Fortunately for
the fellow's morning slumber, Longarm's boots were well
settled and comfortable now.

There was no packing to do and no luggage to hang onto,
so he picked up his hat and went downstairs. The hotel had a
dining room, but it was not open yet, so he went out onto the
porch, stood there for a moment to get his bearings, and
headed for the friendly café where he had eaten the day before. This time it was open. There were already half a dozen
customers sitting at the counter, and two more at one of the
tables.

The same woman was waiting tables this morning as
had waited on him yesterday. She greeted him with a smile
of welcome. "Good morning, sir. It's nice to see you back."
She even sounded like she meant it.

"Got any more of that rhubarb pie?" he asked as he slid
onto a stool at the counter.

"Always when it's in season."

"I'd like a big slab o' that then. No, make it two. And
something for breakfast. What d'you have?"

"Hotcakes. Sausage. Coffee. Pork chops."

Longarm nodded. "Ayuh, that sounds fine."

"All of it?"

He nodded again and smiled.

"I do like to see a hungry man eat. I'll be right back with
your pie and coffee while we fix the rest of your meal."

By the time he'd wrapped himself around his breakfast,
Longarm felt like a new man. His belly was warm from the
inside out and he felt fit as a gray wolf in lambing season.

He felt so good, in fact, that he left fifty cents to pay for a twenty-five-cent meal.

"Thank you, ma'am," he said with a tip of his hat to the lady behind the counter.

"Thank *you*! Have a fine day now."

He saw a barbershop that opened early—or not so very early by now, as the sun was well up and climbing—and went in. There was only one customer ahead of him, so he sat and picked up a local newspaper to glance through while he waited.

A shave, a trim around the ears and his nose, and he would be set for the day. But not his mustache. Nobody touched Longarm's mustache but himself.

He turned the page and read another article. It seemed the city council was considering an ordinance to require that all dogs be contained behind fences as too many accidents were being caused by stray dogs nipping at the heels of dray horses.

Longarm smiled silently to himself. He did not think he had felt this good in a long time.

Chapter 21

Delbert Schrank turned out to be a younger man than Longarm expected—twenty-three according to his booking sheet—with longish hair and a vacant expression. Longarm suspected the young man was not the sharpest knife in the drawer.

He was big, though. Almost as tall as Longarm and much more heavily muscled. Like an ox, Longarm thought. He had hair as black as an Indian's and at least a week's worth of beard growth, which he kept digging at with his fingernails as best he could with his wrists in cuffs.

The Omaha desk officer, a corporal Longarm had not seen before, brought Schrank out in manacles. He handed the key to Longarm and said, "Sign here." Longarm did, and the corporal leaned forward across his desk so he could get a better look at this federal deputy.

"Maybe it ain't none of my business, Deputy, but would you like the borrow of a stout ol' hickory club?"

"Now, why in the world would I need a thing like that?" Longarm asked.

"To keep this sorry son of a bitch in line, that's what.

The big bastard can be a handful, but he's not too stupid to learn a thing or two."

Longarm's expression hardened. "Thank you for the advice, but I think him an' me will manage." He turned to Schrank and said, "Come along, Delbert."

"Yes, sir, Boss."

Longarm looked at him closely, then said, "I'm not your boss, son. Just a deputy marshal escorting you back to Denver."

They stepped out onto the sidewalk, and Schrank tipped his head back to the sun and breathed deeply. "Feels good to be out of doors again."

"How long you been in there?"

"Seventeen days, four hours, and I'd guess, twenty minutes or so."

"Guess?"

Schrank grinned. "Okay, so maybe I noticed the clock on the wall back there."

Longarm laughed. "Looka here now. That beard looks like it's got to the itching stage. We got time before the train leaves. Would you like a shave?"

"Would I? Lordy, I reckon. But I don't have no money, sir. You should know that."

"I have a little. I'll cover you."

Longarm retraced his path to the barbershop where he had gotten his shave just a little while earlier. The place was fairly busy now, with one customer in the chair and another three waiting. Longarm chose a seat close to the door and motioned Schrank into the chair next to his.

"Sir?"

"Mmm?"

"Could I ask you something, sir?"

"You can ask anything. Whether I answer depends on what

you ask. If I do answer, I can promise it'll be the truth," Longarm said.

"Could I ask you . . . that is . . . where are you taking me, sir, and why?"

"They didn't tell you?"

Schrank shook his head. "No, sir. Not a word."

Longarm explained the situation to him.

"What if I don't want to testify against Matt's brother?" Schrank squirmed in his chair. Longarm guessed he might have picked up some lice in that jail cell. Such a thing was not unheard of.

"That would be entirely up to you, Delbert."

"Call me Del, sir. Most do."

Longarm nodded and went on. "The prosecutor in Denver will try to pressure you into testifying, but there's only so much he can do. Of course he'll explain that he can prosecute you for taking those stamps. That would mean maybe as much as five years in prison if you're convicted."

"What if I'm not guilty, sir?"

Longarm smiled and slapped the young fellow's knee. "I said if you're *convicted*, Del. I didn't say nothing about if you're guilty."

"Oh." Schrank paused for a moment, then said, "Yes, I see the difference."

"Me, I don't care one way or the other," Longarm said. "I'm just taking you back to where there's a federal court with jurisdiction. In the meantime, if you're straight with me, I'll be fine with you. I got no reason to have hard feelings for you, an' I won't unless you up an' give me some."

"I'll try not to do that, sir. I didn't set out to be a vexation to nobody."

Longarm nudged Del in the arm. "I think you're up next.

Get your shave, a haircut too if you want one, then . . . are you hungry?"

"I could eat a rattlesnake raw, buzz buttons and all, then pick my teeth with the fangs."

"I know a nice café where we can stuff some food down your gullet."

Schrank brightened. He looked genuinely pleased, despite the reason for this journey.

Chapter 22

Longarm drained his coffee cup and set it down. Schrank was just about finished with his second platter of bacon and eggs. The young fellow acted like he was about half-starved. Apparently the Omaha jail wasted no money on food for their prisoners. Enough to keep them barely alive was deemed enough.

"Finished?" Longarm asked when Schrank finally laid down his fork and sat back from the table. He had been hunched over his plate like a hen guarding her chicks. Now he seemed contented. He looked at Longarm and nodded. "That was good. Thanks."

"You're my prisoner. My responsibility," Longarm said.

Schrank smiled. "Funny thing, I don't much feel like a prisoner."

"If it'll make you feel any better, I can put handcuffs on you. Might even be able to borrow some leg irons from the locals. You can wear 'em all the way back to Denver."

The prisoner laughed. "Nice of you to offer. If I decide I want them, I'll let you know."

"Fair enough," Longarm told him. "In the meantime let's

head over to the depot. I want you to help me get some baggage aboard the train when it's ready to load."

"I'll be glad to help, sir."

Longarm paid for the meal and made a mental note of the cost. That was an expense he would be reimbursed for later. Henry never balked at approving payment for legitimate prisoner upkeep.

Schrank led the way outside but stopped just beyond the doorway. He seemed to be staring off down the street at something. Longarm stepped up beside him. "Something wrong?"

"I thought. . . ." Schrank paused, then shook his head. "Nothing, I guess. Nothing's wrong."

"This way then," Longarm said, nudging Schrank into motion.

They walked over to the Union Pacific depot and around to the freight storage area at the far side of the building.

A train sat waiting on the tracks, already made up and softly hissing steam. Passengers were gathered on the platform, some of them surrounded by friends or family, others standing in the solitude of an anonymous crowd.

"Oh, shit," Longarm muttered.

"Something wrong?"

"Yes, dammit, I forgot t'bring anything for the cat to eat."

"Cat? You have a pet cat?"

"It's not mine, it . . . it's a long story. I'll explain later."

"Whatever you say."

"Help me put the cage aboard, then we'll go fetch something for the critter to eat an' drink."

Minutes later Longarm and his prisoner climbed down from the baggage car and started back toward the café, where Longarm figured they could get a chunk of meat or some such for the cat to eat and maybe an empty tin can to carry water for the animal. In front of them on the platform a man who had been heading toward the freight office spun around and went the other way, tugging his hat brim down as if to cover his face. Odd, Longarm thought. But then people can appear to be strange for the damnedest reasons. Or for none at all.

The waitress at the café gave them a whole chicken breast once Longarm told her what the meat was to be for. No charge, she insisted, saying the breast had fallen on the floor and could not be served to customers anyway. Longarm suspected she was lying, probably a cat lover like Mrs. Vail's friend, but there was nothing wrong with that, he supposed. No harm done.

She also contributed a full can of milk, as well as an empty milk can with water in it. She did not charge them for the milk and offered no pretenses about that having fallen on the floor.

"Thanks." There was no charge, but Longarm left her a quarter for her kindness.

"People are nice, aren't they?" Schrank said as they once again emerged from the café.

"Mostly," Longarm said. "In my business a man tends to forget that from time to time, but it's true. Most are good folks. It's just the occasional asshole that puts a blot on things. Hurry it up, Del. I think they're boarding the westbound now."

Chapter 23

As soon as Del Schrank stepped onto the sun-grayed boards of the sidewalk in front of the café, he screamed, "Watch out!" and threw himself facedown.

Longarm heard the dull boom of a gunshot and the thump of a lead slug striking something solid. It sounded like it hit wood, though, not flesh.

He dropped into a crouch and, Colt in hand, peered around the doorjamb.

A man wearing a calfskin vest and black Kossuth hat stood on the sidewalk half a block away. He had a pistol in hand. A puff of white gunsmoke hung in the still air near him.

"Drop it," Longarm shouted.

Instead the man swung the muzzle of his revolver toward Longarm.

Longarm's Colt bucked in his hand, and smoke and flame burst out of the barrel. The shooter darted to the side and disappeared into an alley.

"Shit," Longarm muttered. "I musta missed him. Are you hit, Del?"

"Uh . . . no. I don't think so." Schrank's voice was shaky and weak, but Longarm put that down to fear not incapacity.

"Go back inside the café. Stay there till I come for you. If it's the guy that shot at you who walks in, run like hell."

Without waiting for an answer, Longarm took off running toward the mouth of the alley where the shooter had gone. He stopped short of it though. Only a fool bursts headlong into an opening where an armed enemy might lie in wait.

He brought his Colt up shoulder high, took a deep breath, and eased slowly forward until he could get a look into the alley. All he saw there was the usual litter of discarded cans and broken crates.

He stepped fully into the alley mouth for a better look, but he had no target there.

The shooter could not be very far ahead, so Longarm ran forward, going to the back of the building that housed the café and four other Omaha businesses.

To his left, off in the direction of the railroad depot, he caught a glimpse of the back of the fleeing gunman's vest. Longarm took off after him.

The son of a bitch was not the best shot in the world—after all, he had missed a good chance at Del Schrank—but he could run like a damn rabbit. It was all Longarm could do to keep him in sight as he darted this way and that through alleys and around businesses, until he reached the maze of tracks in the railroad yard, where Longarm soon lost him.

Dozens of passenger cars, stock cars, freight cars, and flatbeds lay singly or in short strings waiting to be made up into trains. The roundhouse held one of the U.P.'s huge engines, silent now with its fires pulled and steam down. Half a dozen railroad men stood staring after the shooter, or at least Longarm hoped that was what they were staring at. He ran in that direction.

He might well have run on by and missed the SOB, but the flare of a muzzle flash blossomed in the deep shade of the covered roundhouse. A slug sizzled over Longarm's head. Nope. Bastard was not much for accuracy in his shooting. Not that Longarm was complaining about that.

He held his fire and charged straight toward the cavernous opening to the roundhouse.

The shot had come from just to the left of the engine on the roundhouse cradle.

Longarm moved to his left just in time to see the shooter's back as he ran out the other side of the roundhouse. Longarm took a gamble and ran as hard as he could around the north side.

He grunted with satisfaction as he saw the gunman scramble into sight behind the big building and run back toward him. The shooter had expected Longarm to enter the roundhouse in pursuit. And it was already clear that the fellow had a tendency to go to his left when given a choice.

You lose, he thought to himself as the shooter, seeing Longarm standing in front of him, skidded to a halt, slipped on the loose gravel and cinders, and almost lost his footing.

"Drop it," Longarm shouted. "You're under arrest."

Instead the gunman, a panicky look on his face, raised his pistol in Longarm's direction.

Longarm triggered his Colt and then again. His first bullet took the man low in the belly, doubling him over and dropping him to his knees. The second probably would have struck in the same place as the first except that by then the gunman himself was lower. The second slug slammed into the top of the man's head. Brain matter squirted out of his ears and blood flowed from his nose and mouth.

Whatever this had been about, and why he was shooting at Delbert Schrank, the prisoner had nothing to fear from the fellow now.

Longarm took a moment to pull a handful of cartridges from his coat pocket and reload the Colt, then he started slowly back toward the café. He needed to get Schrank back into custody, then notify the Omaha police about the shooting if they did not already know.

Probably, dammit, they would have some reports for him to fill out too. The cops here did seem to like their paperwork.

Chapter 24

Once things calmed down, with all the forms filled out and reports written and signed, Longarm took Schrank by the elbow and pulled him into a small room at the police head-quarters. The room was ordinarily used for the interrogation of suspects ... which was pretty much what Longarm intended to use it for now.

"You an' me need to talk," he told his young prisoner. "That dead fella. You knew him."

"I . . ."

"Don't be tryin' to deny it. He's what you shied away from when we was coming out of the eatery this afternoon, and that was him in the crowd on the platform later on. He was laying for you, Delbert. He didn't try and ask you any-thing or warn you about anything, he just started throwing lead in your direction. If you hadn't thrown yourself down like you done, you likely would be the dead man laying over there in a box. So ... who the fuck was that fella?"

Schrank stared at his toes for a bit and squirmed on his chair. He craned his neck to look around, but the walls of the interrogation room were as bare as a fifty-cent whore's ass. There was nothing to look at except the man who sat across the table boring holes in Schrank's head with the fixed look he was giving him.

Finally Schrank looked at Longarm again. "I don't know his name. I seen him a couple times before."

"With the Jennings bunch?"

Schrank looked down again, twisting his fingers together and wringing his hands like he expected to squeeze water out of them. In a very small voice he said, "Yes, sir. With Mattie's brother an' them."

"Did you ever ride with that bunch yourself?"

Schrank quickly looked into Longarm's eyes again. "No, sir. Never. I knew them, through Matt, but I never rode with them. Not when they were . . . you know. Working."

"You knew what they were doing when they rode off?"

Schrank shrugged.

"Is that a yes?"

"All right, dammit. Yes. I knew."

"You didn't say anything."

"It wasn't my job to. And anyway Matt is my friend. I wouldn't want to get him in trouble."

"Now you are in trouble, Delbert, and your only way out of it is to testify to what you know about Matt Jennings and his brother and the brother's gang."

Schrank shrugged again.

"I'm gonna tell you something else, Delbert, in case you haven't figured it out for your own self," Longarm said in a calm, level voice. "Your friend Matt and his brother have decided they can't trust you. They don't want you to live long enough to get up on that witness stand and swear to tell the truth. They're afraid you just might actually do that and the truth would land all o' them in prison. They'd rather see you dead than take a chance on you."

"I know that. You're right." Schrank leaned back and stared toward the ceiling. After a moment he said, "You know the funny thing?"

Longarm grunted.

"When I get to Denver and they put me on the stand, I was going to say I never saw anything, didn't know anything about Mattie or his brother or what the gang might've been up to."

"But you do know, don't you?"

Schrank nodded. "When they came back, they were drunk on the fun of it all. They didn't really need the liquor they put down after a robbery. They'd drink and laugh and brag on who did what and how much they took. They told it all and nobody cared that I was listening because I was Matt's pal and wouldn't say anything." Schrank gave a small, snorting laugh. "And I didn't. Not a word, not to anybody. Till now." He stood. "Look, it's getting late and I'm hungry and I'm tired and I'd like to get the hell out of this place if you don't mind."

Longarm stood too. Schrank held his wrists out, obviously expecting Longarm to put handcuffs on him now.

"What's that for?" Longarm asked.

"I thought . . . well, you know."

"What I know is that you could've tried to run while I was busy chasing after that sonuvabitch. You didn't. I'm no more inclined to put manacles on you now than I was before."

"Thank you, sir. And for what it's worth, I give you my word I won't try and run on you. I'll go to Denver with you. When the time comes, I'll testify."

Longarm nodded. "Your word is good enough for me, son. And by the way, you'll have to testify twice, first before a grand jury to get indictments against the gang and then again when they're caught and go on trial. I don't know if anybody's made that clear to you, but that's the way it will play out."

"Whatever it takes," Schrank said. "I'm not spending any time in prison for somebody that tried to have me shot down in the street like that."

"All right." Longarm smiled. "Now let's you and me go find a room for the night . . . Damn westbound is long since gone an' I don't know yet when there'll be another. We'll find us a room and a bite to eat and . . . Oh, shit." Longarm slapped himself on the forehead and said, "My bag, all my stuff. And the damn cat. We got t' go over to the depot quick and wire ahead for them to take the cage and my bag off at Grand Island."

Longarm yanked the door open and took off at a run toward the Union Pacific depot. Del Schrank followed behind as close as he could.

Chapter 25

"Sorry, sir." The telegrapher looked up at the clock on the wall as if to double-check his information, then at a routing book. "It's too late to have them off-load your goods at Grand Island." He looked at Longarm and smiled, trying to be helpful. "But I can have them taken off for you at Julesburg."

"Oh, jeez," Longarm moaned.

"Do you want me to do that, sir?"

"Yes. Yes, dammit, I want you to do that."

"Right away, sir." The telegrapher turned away and went to his key.

Longarm walked back a few paces so he could get a better look at the schedule board. There would be another westbound at 2:15 in the morning and again at 10:12. A third would go at 3:40 P.M. The middle-of-the-night train would carry freight only; the others were mixed freight and passenger.

It really made no difference to him. As a deputy United States marshal, he could ride in the caboose of a pure freight if he chose. On the other hand . . . 2:15 A.M. was a miserable time to get up for or to stay awake for, either one.

Dammit!

He had to think about his prisoner *and* that damned cat. He turned to Schrank, who was patiently waiting nearby. "Reckon we're stuck here till morning. We'll get us a room an' something to eat, then maybe a bottle. It wouldn't be right for me to take a prisoner to inspect the saloons in this town . . . excuse me, I think they call them 'bars' here, like as if that makes some sorta difference. That wouldn't be right, and I damn sure ain't putting you back in that jail tonight, so I guess the best thing will be for us t'do any relaxing by ourselves in the hotel room. Not exciting but sensible. Are you a drinking man, Delbert?"

"I been known to enjoy a drink now and then," the young prisoner said. "And, um, Longarm . . . I want you to know I appreciate you not sending me back into that cell. The guards there aren't hardly human, the way they treat people. The prisoners that can't pay them for special services, that is."

Longarm's eyebrows went up.

"Tobacco, whiskey, decent food . . . you wouldn't believe the shit they serve there . . . things like that. Rumor was that the long-term prisoners could even get a woman if they had the coin to cover it, but I don't know that for a fact. I was housed in the transient section. They was a floor higher than me."

"I hate to tell you this, son, but I ain't exactly shocked," Longarm said. "That sorta shit goes on. Most everyplace, I guess."

"It's a shame, isn't it," Schrank observed.

"That it is, but there's nothing you or me can do about it, so our best bet is to avoid it and do what we think is right."

"Yes, sir."

"Now, let's you and me go check into the hotel and then find us some supper. We'll just take things as they come."

Chapter 26

The steam-driven engine rolled across the vast expanses of Nebraska spewing coal smoke and cinders, stopping every so often to drop off freight or take some aboard. Longarm sat in the smoking car savoring a cheroot while Del Schrank dozed on the seat beside him. They had not bothered to get off at Grand Island, but rumbled on to Julesburg. It was nearly morning again when the conductor came through to shake them both awake.

"You said you wanted Julesburg right, Marshal?" he asked softly so as to not disturb passengers who were traveling on to the west.

"I did. Thanks." Longarm took Schrank by the shoulder and jostled him. "Rise and shine, Del."

"Where we?" Schrank muttered sleepily. "Denver?" He blinked rapidly and rubbed his eyes.

"Julesburg. We got to recover that damn cat here. And my carpetbag. I can't forget that."

"Mm, sure." Schrank yawned and stretched his arms out wide. "You got anything left in that bottle?"

Longarm shook his head. "Sorry. We killed that sonu-vabitch last night."

Schrank grinned. "Maybe, but it put up a good fight while it lasted."

Longarm chuckled and stood, lifting his Stetson to allow a little fresh air to reach his scalp, and then tugging the hat back in place. "Ready?"

Schrank nodded. "Lead the way."

Longarm stepped down to the platform—not very busy at this hour—and asked a passing railroad crewman where he could find the freight office. In reponse the man in striped coveralls and a large bandana pointed down the platform past the ticket office and telegrapher. "Thanks."

He had to rap on the Dutch door four times, each knock louder than the last, before he roused anyone inside.

"Yeah?"

Longarm identified himself and said, "I'm here to pick up one bag and a cage with a black cat in it."

"Not here," the freight agent said.

"But it has to be. Are you sure? I was told—"

"Mister, I ain't lying to you so don't get all het up about it. I had your cat. The bag too. But we got a wire from someplace down the line. Omaha maybe. Said the cat and the bag was supposed to be in Grand Island. So I sent them back." The fellow turned and checked the time on the wall clock. "If they ain't there yet, they real soon will be."

"Well, shit," Longarm snarled.

"Sorry, mister." He did not sound it, however.

"All right, so when is the next eastbound?" Longarm asked.

"We got a passenger coming through in about four hours."

"Nothing sooner?"

"There's a freight, but . . ."

"We'll take it," Longarm said.

"Mister, passengers got to ride in passenger coaches. I'm sorry." This time he sounded like he might actually mean what he said.

Longarm pulled out his wallet and flipped it open to show the badge inside. "We'll ride in the caboose."

"Yes, sir, Marshal. Let me tell the boss. I'll tell the conductor soon as the train pulls in."

Chapter 27

The Union Pacific freight rumbled across the rolling plains of Nebraska. Again. In the other direction. Longarm and Del Schrank sat on the bare, unpadded wood of the benches installed in the caboose. Brakemen came and went, entering the caboose to eat their lunches or gulp down a dipper of water from the barrel at the back of the car. They ignored the passengers except for an occasional mumbled hello as they passed.

Shortly after midday the freight stopped at Grand Island. "Don't dawdle," the obviously annoyed conductor told them. "We wouldn't have to stop here except for you two. You're going to screw up our schedule if you take too long, so don't. Otherwise we'll go on even if you're still aboard."

"A quick stop is all we need," Longarm said. "C'mon, Del."

He led the way onto the small, railed platform at the rear of the caboose, and they waited there until the train came to a squealing halt as the brakemen did their jobs. As soon as the huge vehicle was slow enough, Longarm swung down off the steel ladder, stepping down onto the trackside gravel, with Schrank close behind.

The conductor leaned out from the side of the car and signaled the engineer, whose station was a good quarter mile forward, in the massive steam engine. It took only moments for the train to begin surging ahead again. It quickly gathered speed and soon was disappearing toward the east.

The point where Longarm and Del Schrank left the train was about a hundred yards west of the Grand Island depot where the cat cage should be waiting. They started walking toward it.

"Ah!" Schrank cried out and fell to the ground.

For a moment Longarm thought the man had simply tripped and fallen. Then, seconds afterward, he heard the dull boom of a rifle shot.

There on the far side of the depot he saw a puff of white gunsmoke.

His prisoner, the man Longarm was charged with escorting back to Denver so he could testify in federal court, had been shot.

Colt in hand, Longarm began racing toward the rapidly dissipating telltale smoke.

Chapter 28

Longarm heard the bumblebee zip of a bullet passing close by his head and again saw the puff of pale smoke from the shooter's rifle.

Rifle. Dammit! All Longarm had was his Colt revolver. The rifleman had much greater range with his weapon. Longarm had to get closer if he wanted a good shot at the man. Ideally he would want to do that while remaining alive and unpunctured himself.

He zigzagged left and right.

Another puff of smoke that was quickly followed by the sound of gunshot. He had no idea where that bullet went. The man up there obviously was not an expert marksman. He might be—probably was—a piece of shit and a blot on society, but he was not an accomplished rifleman.

Not that Custis Long was complaining.

He angled to his left, trying to place the solid bulk of the railroad depot between himself and the shooter. Seconds afterward he darted to his right again.

And grinned, the expression wicked with satisfaction.

Just as he hoped, the shooter made a break out of his

hidden position as soon as he thought Longarm would run
around the north side of the depot.

Longarm got a good look at him as he bolted for the
block of businesses that lined the street between the depot
and the town.

Medium height. Red checked shirt. Light-colored hat in
a Montana peak.

And no rifle. Apparently he had ditched the rifle so he
could make a quicker and more believable getaway.

Not gonna work, buddy, Longarm thought as he redou-
bled his efforts, running all out now, with no need to zigzag.

The shooter darted into the back door of a business building.

Longarm angled sharply to his right, his breath coming
ragged now, but he was determined that the son of a bitch
not get away from him.

He burst out onto the street in time to see the shooter run
out the front door of whatever business he'd run through.

The would-be assassin did not look back, obviously thinking he had successfully escaped from Longarm's pursuit.
Instead he pushed his hands into his pockets and slowed to a
nonchalant saunter along the sidewalk.

He must have thought he had gotten away clean until he
heard Longarm's pounding footsteps coming up fast behind.

He turned then and his eyes went wide as he recognized
the tall, deadly lawman he had just tried to murder.

He spun away and once again tried to run.

"Halt or I'll shoot," Longarm bellowed.

Several passersby on the street headed for the safety of
shops and doorways.

The shooter ran into the street, heading toward an alley
mouth fifty or sixty feet ahead.

Longarm stopped, raised his Colt, and thumbed the hammer back.

"Halt, damn you."

The shooter made no effort to comply.

Longarm took careful aim at the man's legs and tripped the trigger.

His heaving breath, dammit, ruined the accuracy of his bullet. His .45 slug took the man between his shoulder blades, ripped through his lungs and the lower chambers of his heart, and sent him plunging facedown—and quite thoroughly dead—into the dirt and drying horse shit in the street.

"Oh, shit," Longarm muttered. He had wanted to take this man alive. Wanted to question the bastard.

He would not be getting much information out of the man now.

Longarm turned and began trotting—he was too winded to actually run—back toward Delbert Schrank.

Chapter 29

Del Schrank was sitting on the end of a railroad tie holding a bandana over a bloody hole in his upper left arm.

"Son of a bitch shot me," he declared, stating the obvious. "Why?"

"Well shit, son, I don't expect he done it just for the hell of it," Longarm drawled, struggling to regain his breath and at the same time reaching for a cheroot.

"Did you get him?" Schrank asked.

Longarm nodded. "I wanted to just bring him down so's we could ask him a few things, but my bullet flew high. Bastard's dead."

"Good. But he sure as hell messed up my day."

"Think you can walk?"

Schrank tried to get to his feet, failed, and sat back down. "Help me up, will you?"

"You can wait a spell if you like," Longarm offered.

"No, sir, I'll be all right if you just help me stand up."

Longarm took a little more time than was necessary to nip off the twist on the end of his cigar and get the thing lighted, then he took Del Schrank by the good arm and eased him upright. "How's that?"

"Fine. Just fine, sir."

"Walk beside me, nice an' slow. If you think you're gonna fall down, grab hold of my arm. If we have to, I can bring one o' those baggage carts and wheel you over there."

"Over where?"

Longarm tipped his head in the direction of the dead man lying on the city street. A crowd was already gathered around the corpse. "There," he said. "I want you to get a good look at the guy. See if you might know him. If you do, you might could figure out why he wants you dead." Longarm took a drag on his cheroot. "If it's for anything other than because you're fixing to testify against the Jennings gang. Uh, you *are* still gonna testify against the Jennings bunch, aren't you?"

"Matter of fact, I am. All this shooting and shit kinda made up my mind for me. So yes, I am damn sure going to testify to what I know, and if that gets Mattie in trouble, well, that's the way it is."

"Good man," Longarm said.

When they reached the crowd standing around the dead man, a tall, lanky fellow with a star pinned to his vest stepped out of the bunch. "You are the one who shot this man down?" Longarm noticed that the local lawman had one hand on the butt of his revolver and held a pair of handcuffs in the other.

Longarm reached inside his coat. The lawman awkwardly yanked his revolver out. It was a very old Remington Navy that had been converted to accept modern .38 cartridges. It was also in Longarm's opinion a very poor choice for a town marshal to carry. But then it was already obvious that gunplay was not often required in Grand Island.

"Don't get excited," Longarm said, flipping his wallet open.

"Who . . . ?"

"Deputy U.S. marshal," Longarm said. He identified himself, and the local shoved his pistol back into its leather.

The local officer extended his hand to Longarm and said, "I'm Tim Brightson. Deputy here. If you don't mind, I'm going to want to ask you some questions and get you to fill out a report on this shooting. Would that be all right, Deputy?"

"Sure, whatever you need, but first my prisoner here needs a doctor and he needs to take a look at that dead fella there."

Brightson turned and said, "Billy, go get Doc Hendricks. Tell him to meet us at City Hall. Tell him he has a gunshot to tend."

"Yes, sir," a young fellow in the crowd said with a grin. He took off at a run, presumably to find the doctor and tell him what Brightson needed.

Deputy Brightson shooed most of the crowd away from the dead man and led Schrank to the body.

"Know him?" Longarm asked.

"No, but I've seen him." Schrank looked sad. "I just can't believe Matt would do this to me. I can't believe my friend would wish me dead."

"It's a lousy thing to find out, isn't it."

"Yeah. Yeah, it really is. You think they've put the word out that I'm to be killed?"

"It sure as hell looks that way, don't it," Longarm said.

"If you boys are done looking, we can go over to City Hall. The marshal's office and our jail are in the basement there," Brightson said.

"Sure." Longarm touched Schrank's elbow, the good one,

and asked, "D'you think you can walk some more or do you want to ride on a cart?"

"I can walk." But halfway to the City Hall building, Schrank's legs gave out and he ended up sitting on the edge of a board sidewalk. Brightson sent some kids back to the depot to find a baggage cart and wheel it to them. Schrank made the rest of the journey to City Hall riding on the cart.

The doctor was already there waiting for them.

Chapter 30

"It's mostly loss of blood," the doctor said as he worked over Del Schrank's arm. The doctor was young, probably still in his twenties, with blond hair and china blue eyes. According to Brightson, he was very capable. He used a curved needle and forceps to stitch the gaping wound about four inches above Schrank's left elbow.

Fortunately for Schrank, the rifle bullet had sliced across his arm without encountering bone. Consequently it left only one hole in his flesh, but that was a fairly large one.

"Lose too much blood," the doctor intoned as he worked, "and you lose strength as well. You will be just fine, young man, but you will experience a great deal of pain until this wound is healed. I can give you some laudanum to help you through the pain, and I have an ointment that should speed the healing process." He smiled. "Just be careful to avoid reading the label on the jar. It might upset you to find out that your medicine is normally intended for use on the wounds of horses and other livestock."

"It's kind of a sticky black tar kind of stuff?" Schrank

asked. "I think I know the stuff you mean. Works a charm to heal horses. I've used it before."

"It should work just as well to heal you," Dr. Hendricks assured him. "What about you?" he asked, looking at Longarm. "Were you harmed in this melee?"

"No, I came off scot-free," Longarm said.

"You are in charge of this man?" he asked, indicating Schrank.

"Ayuh. He's my prisoner."

"Well, he needs bed rest for a day or two and fluids. Plenty of fluids to make up for all the blood he has lost." Hendricks finished his sewing project and began packing Schrank's wound with picked lint, then wrapping it with strips of clean linen. "Give him tea. I know, I know, don't tell me. Tea is a lady's drink. It also does wonders to help restore vitality to the blood. Don't ask me why. Above all, avoid spirits. No whiskey or rum, nothing like that. Beer would be acceptable to replace the lost blood."

Schrank grinned and said, "Doc, I think my blood was mostly beer to begin with."

"Then by all means have more. But have the deputy there bring a bucket to you. I don't want you wandering off to visit the saloons or, um, any of the more vigorous amusements available there. I want you propped up in bed. You can have your tea there . . . In fact, I shall send some up to you in the hotel . . . and beer later, after you've started to recuperate."

"Whoa," Longarm said. "Hotel? Are you sayin' we'll be staying for a spell?"

"At least three days," Hendricks told them. "And no cheating. I don't want this man moved until he is building his blood back to where it should be and some of the pain is subsiding." The doctor dropped his stethoscope into his black bag and snapped the bag closed. "Check in at the Ramsgate Hotel. It is directly across the street here. I'll look in on Mr. Schrank from time to time." He looked Longarm in the eye. "Do we understand each other, Deputy?"

"Yes, Doc, I reckon we do."

"Very well then. Come along. I'll get you two settled in the hotel and instruct them to carry a tray up to Mr. Schrank at suppertime." He smiled. "They are accustomed to my instructions. They will see that the patient has bed rest and fluids."

"Yes, sir." Longarm, Hendricks, and the doctor's husky assistant helped Del Schrank across the rutted street to the Ramsgate Hotel and upstairs to an unusually clean room with a cloud-soft feather bed and braided rugs.

"Remember what I told you," Hendricks said after Schrank had been stripped of his clothing and put into bed, where he was practically swallowed up by the mattress and comforter. "No cheating. Fluids and bed rest."

With that, the doctor and his assistant were gone.

"Now what?" Schrank asked.

"You heard the doc. Bed rest an' fluids, that's what."

"For how long?"

"For as long as it takes. A few days, I'd think."

"What about your cat?"

"It ain't my cat, dammit, I've told you that," Longarm snapped. "But . . . thanks for reminding me. I had clean forgot about the little son of a bitch." He looked around the room. "Listen, Del, there's only room enough for one in that bed, so I'm gonna ask for your promise that you won't try to slip away."

"Longarm, I don't want to get away. I'm depending on you to protect me from Luke Jennings. He has to be behind these attempts on my life, and if Luke is anything like Matt, he won't stop until he does what he thinks he has to do."

"All right then. I think you're safe, at least for the time

being. I'm gonna take a room in the hotel too. Then I suppose I'll have to go feed the damn cat."

"Don't forget the sandbox and clean water," Schrank said.

"Yes, dammit, those too." Longarm went out into the hallway and downstairs to check into the hotel himself.

Chapter 31

Del Schrank might be under doctor's orders to avoid going out on the town, but Longarm wasn't. He paid a boy twenty-five cents to take care of the cat and asked at the depot for the best saloon in town.

"Yonder is the closest," the freight agent told him, pointing down the street that ran past the depot, "but the fanciest is in town. Two blocks down and another two over. Called the Holland. It's named for the lady that runs it, not the country."

Longarm's interest suddenly perked up. "A lady named Holland, you say? She wouldn't be BethAnne Holland, would she?"

The freight agent stifled a yawn, then said, "I wouldn't know. The place is too fancy for me. Too expensive too. Ten cents for a beer. Quarter for brandy or a whiskey. No sir, too expensive for a normal man. The Holland caters to the high-muckety-mucks in the county. Bankers, judges, big shots like that."

"That leaves me out too," Longarm said with a smile. But when he left the U.P. depot, it was toward the Holland that he immediately went.

The Holland Tavern was a two-story affair with a gilded gingerbread false front and brightly burning gaslights inside. Instead of ordinary batwings, the entrance was through double doors with glass panels set into them.

Through the doors there was soft music provided by a piano, a violin, and a string bass. There was a bar, but it was fairly short and attended by a bartender but no patrons. The customers, half a dozen of them all wearing suit coats, sat at tables. Four exceptionally attractive, and quite nicely dressed, young women waited on the tables. Longarm assumed that the girls provided more than just food and drink to the customers.

He walked over to the bar, which he noticed did not even have a foot rail, nor were there any cuspidors on the floor, although there were heavy glass ashtrays on the tables. Apparently a man was expected to smoke here but not chew.

The bartender, a handsome young man with mustaches almost as luxuriant as Longarm's, immediately came down the length of the bar to meet him. "Welcome, sir. Would you care to have a seat at one of our tables, please. One of your ladies will bring your drink order to me."

"Maybe I'll do that in a minute," Longarm said, "but I'm mostly here to inquire about BethAnne."

"Pardon me, sir?"

"BethAnne Holland. I'm lookin' for her."

"I am sure I don't know what you mean, sir," the barman said. "Would you care for something to drink? Perhaps a meal? We have food too, you see."

"BethAnne," Longarm insisted. "I want to see her."

"I am sorry, sir." The bartender turned away and went to the other end of the bar.

A voice from upstairs called, "Rye whiskey for the gentleman, Jimmy, and an order of oysters on the half shell. You can have them served in my rooms."

Longarm looked up and grinned. "Nice t'see you doin' so well these days, BethAnne."

"It's nice to see you too, Custis. Now, come up here and join me. You can tell me all about your latest adventures."

He practically ran up the stairs to join her.

Chapter 32

BethAnne greeted him with a friendly hug. And with a kiss that had her tongue halfway down Longarm's throat. He did not object. He knew what other marvelous things that tongue could do.

"How long has it been, Custis? Ten years? Fifteen?" she asked once she had the use of her own tongue back.

He smiled. "Too long. The time's been good to you though. You haven't changed a bit." It was a lie, but a kind one. BethAnne now was still a handsome woman. When last he'd seen her she was a stunning one.

BethAnne was an orphan. She'd run away from an abusive orphanage at a very early age—she hadn't been willing to admit to just how early—and nearly starved before she learned that her beauty could be used as a commodity.

After experiencing the perils of rape several times over, she showed up on the doorstep of the finest whorehouse in her town—the name of that town being another detail she preferred to keep to herself—and announced herself willing to work there.

She discovered that being fucked for money involved

strange men just as smelly and unpleasant as the ones who
raped her. And for not much more money. The house kept
nearly all the money she earned.

BethAnne was not satisfied with that life, so on a day off
from her whorehouse duties she seduced the manager of a
traveling troupe of entertainers and let the man know that he
would continue to receive that sort of attention if he would
hire her as part of the troupe.

She had never sung a note before that time, but she immediately became a singer. It was a fortuitous choice because the group discovered, along with BethAnne herself,
that she had a lovely if untutored voice. Between her beauty
and her singing, BethAnne added to the revenue of the
troupe. Resentment of her in the troupe, as the boss's mistress, faded and she became respected as the principal draw.

It was as a singer that Longarm first knew BethAnne.
She was the experienced and beautiful "older woman" to
the young cowboy, and she taught him how to make love to
a woman rather than just fuck her. Their relationship was
not one of love, but it certainly was one of great liking. It
might well have continued into something more except that
her boss and lover found out about them. Instead of causing
a scene, the man merely took his troupe and moved on,
BethAnne among them.

Longarm had not seen or heard of her since.

Now he wrapped his arms around her and kissed her long
and deep.

Nothing had changed in the way he felt about BethAnne
Holland.

Chapter 33

"You used to have the softest, prettiest yellow hair I ever saw," Longarm mused as he sat holding BethAnne on his lap, one hand idly petting her. "How come you dyed it red? I mean . . . it looks good. Don't get me wrong. But I'm just, you know, curious."

She ducked her face close against the side of his neck, her breath warm and pleasant there. "There aren't ten people on God's green earth that I'd tell this to, Custis, but you are one of them. The truth is that I started dying it to get rid of the gray."

Longarm laughed and kissed her again.

"It isn't funny," BethAnne protested. "It was *awful*! Perfectly awful."

"If you say so." He began nibbling on her earlobe. "But I bet you'd look mighty good with gray hair. A real beauty. Which you already are."

"I would look horrid and I know it."

"If you say so," he repeated, "but you're a young woman still." His hand found her right breast and gently caressed it.

"Custis, you know better." BethAnne sighed. "It isn't

something I would normally admit, but dear, I turned fifty last month. Can you believe it? Fifty!"

"An' prettier than ever." He began the pleasant task of unbuttoning her dress.

"Do you want me to help you with that?"

"No, thanks," he said. "I'm enjoyin' myself here, so leave me be, woman." He reached the last button and spread the cloth wide, exposing frilly underthings.

"Just a minute, dear. Let me stand up." BethAnne rose, slipped the dress off her shoulders, and let it fall to the floor.

"Keep goin'. I like the view," he told her.

BethAnne made one theatrical pose after another for him, standing in her undergarments and then slowly, one item at a time, shedding them until all she wore was a garter belt and white stockings.

"Oh, my," Longarm said appreciatively. "You're as gorgeous today as you was then." It was not really a lie, or anyway not much of one. BethAnne's body had thickened a little. Her breasts were heavier and pointed now toward the floor where they used to aim at the sky. He could see a tracery of blue veins beneath skin that once was flawless white. The areolae around her nipples now were the size of silver dollars; they had been like quarters. And her nipples were bigger too.

Longarm leaned forward and took one of those nipples into his mouth, sucking on it gently while one hand circled around behind and stroked the small of her back.

BethAnne encouraged him with both hands pressing against the back of his head. She arched her back and shuddered as the sensations at her nipple brought her to a quick, small climax. "Lovely," she whispered. "You've just gotten better over the years, Custis."

"Let's see if that's true." He stood and took her by the hand, leading her to the big, canopied bed in her room.

"Don't move," BethAnne said.

"Something wrong?"

"Oh, no, dear. I want the pleasure of undressing you, that's all."

Longarm smiled. And stood quiet and still while BethAnne stripped the clothes from him, carefully laying aside his gunbelt and following it with everything else, until he was naked.

"I forgot what a marvelous cock you have," she said.

"I don't think it's changed much. The question is, can you still get it all in your mouth?"

BethAnne chuckled and dropped to her knees.

She could, they were both pleased to discover.

"God, you're a stallion," BethAnne said two hours later as they lay side by side, resting up for another round of belly bumping. Both were slippery with sweat and other delightful fluids. BethAnne's hand idly toyed with the soft skin on Longarm's scrotum.

"An' you're quite a filly," he told her with a smile.

BethAnne sighed. "What a wonderful surprise this is, running into you after all these years."

"Indeed it is, ma'am."

"May I ask you something, dear?"

"Anything." He was wrapping a strand of her hair around and around his index finger then twirling it back in the other direction.

"What are you doing these days? You don't dress like a cowhand anymore. But you don't look exactly like a businessman either. Are you a cattle buyer or something like that?"

He laughed. "Neither o' those. I'm a deputy U.S. marshal. I work outta Denver now."

"A deputy. That sounds exciting. I. . . . Oh, God!" She

sat bolt upright on the bed, a look of concern suddenly on her face.

"Something wrong?"

"Custis, your last name is Long, isn't it?"

"Sure."

"You wouldn't . . . you wouldn't be called Long Arm, would you?"

"Longarm. Yeah, that's me. Like in the long arm o' the law. Or other places."

"Oh, dear, I . . . Custis, dear. I . . . I hear things. You know. A bar, even an upper-class one like this . . . we tend to hear things. And my girls . . . men tell them things. They gossip. And the girls tell me. I encourage that. Information can be so valuable. This . . . Lately, dear, there is word spreading that a deputy named Longarm and his prisoner are on the move in Nebraska. Someone has posted a bounty on them. On *you*! Someone wants you dead, Custis. Someone is willing to pay a thousand dollars to see you and this prisoner dead."

Longarm sat up beside her and put a protective arm around fifty-year-old BethAnne Holland. "Thanks for tellin' me, darlin'. Now I know t' watch my back even more than usual." He smiled. "But whatever happens in the future, it won't affect you an' me tonight. An' I think if you was t'play with that pecker just a little bit more, it'd stand up an' we could have us some more fun. So what do you say, girl? Are you willin'?"

"With you, Custis? Always."

"That's my girl." He bent his head and kissed her. He could taste their juices, hers and his alike, in BethAnne's pretty mouth. His cock did indeed rise to the occasion, and he pressed BethAnne down onto her back. He was smiling as he did so.

Chapter 34

"How're you feelin', Del?"

"I'm breathing. Hurt like hell though. Is something wrong?"

Longarm shook his head. "No, of course not," he lied. He was tired. He'd spent the night sitting in a chair that was leaned up against the door to Schrank's hotel room, a thousand dollars being one hell of a lot of money. That seemed to be what the Jennings boys were willing to pay to stay out of jail.

Shit, if he were in trouble and had a thousand dollars to spend, it would not be spent to hire a murder. That would only dig the hole deeper. No, better to use five hundred of it to hire a big city lawyer, he thought. And with a grin, he added to himself that the remaining five hundred should be spent to bribe a judge. Sad to say there were a few who could be bought if the price was right.

That was not going to happen here, though. And no son of a bitch was going to collect the thousand-dollar bounty on Delbert Schrank. It was typical of the man that Longarm's concern was for his prisoner and not himself.

Now Schrank was awake and Longarm was quite frankly hoping he felt well enough to travel.

He did not. That became obvious when Longarm saw the pain drawing his features into a taut mask and turning his flesh gray.

"Was there something you wanted, Longarm?"

"Yeah," he said. "I was wantin' to see how you are this morning."

"Better, I think. Thanks for asking."

"You bet. I, uh, I'll carry your tray up to you in a little while."

Schrank nodded and closed his eyes. He had some distance to go before he could be considered recovered. But then the bullet that ripped through his flesh had taken a considerable amount of meat and blood with it. The wound was an ugly one, and a man did not just jump back into the saddle after taking a slug like that.

Longarm went downstairs and looked in on the cook. He was pleased with what he saw. She seemed a decent sort of matron. Of course cooks and waiters could use an extra thousand dollars, he was sure. But a man has to trust someone.

Even so, he stood idling in the doorway, keeping one eye on the staircase leading up to Schrank's room and the other on the cook as she prepared breakfast.

"If you don't mind," Longarm said, "I'll carry his meal an' mine up on a tray."

"Ja, mister," the cook said with a smile. She had a thick German accent and a thick waist to go with it. She went on about her business.

Lordy, Longarm mused, he hoped Schrank would not be too long recuperating. He needed to get that cat . . . Oh, shit. The cat. He needed to find someone to tend the little bastard while they were laid over in Grand Island.

He hoped to hell that Billy Vail appreciated all this.

Chapter 35

Breakfast was a treat. Rolled oat porridge, bacon, and flap-
jacks that the German woman managed somehow to make
fluffy and exotic, even with the bacon grease liberally poured
over them. Schrank ate sitting propped up against the head-
board while Longarm balanced his plate on his knees.

"Want some coffee?" Longarm offered when they were
done. "I have to carry the dirty dishes downstairs anyway."

"Sure, I'd like some and the thundermug," Schrank said.

"Think you can manage that by yourself?"

Schrank gave him a dirty look. "Deputy, I've been piss-
ing and shitting without anybody's help for a good long
while now. I think I can manage again this time."

"All right. I'll be right back."

Longarm went downstairs, but instead of grabbing the
coffee and going back up to Schrank's room, he beckoned
the tousle-haired kid who was hanging around the desk.
"Get Marshal Brightson for me. Tell him I need to speak
with him." Longarm handed the boy a nickel and the kid
grinned. "Yes, sir, Marshal, right away, sir."

Longarm got two cups and a steaming hot pot of coffee

and carried them upstairs on a tray along with a can of condensed milk and a cup of sugar. He and Schrank were nearly finished with their first invigorating cups when Tim Brightson showed up.

"What can I do for you, Longarm?"

"I need a favor, Tim. I'd suspect you have some spare artillery layin' around, stuff you've taken from prisoners now an' then."

The local man nodded rather reluctantly. "I might," he conceded.

"I need the borrow of a gun and holster. Something with a belt to fit a good-sized man."

Brightson's eyebrows went up.

"Someone," Longarm continued, "about his size." He hooked a thumb toward Del Schrank.

This time Schrank's eyebrows rose.

"The man is a prisoner, right?"

"Uh-huh."

"You know what you're doing?"

"I think so."

"All right. But it's on your head if anything goes wrong."

"I wouldn't have it no other way," Longarm told him.

Brightson eyed Schrank for a moment, then said, "I think I have something he could use. I'll send it right over."

"I appreciate that, Marshal." When Brightson was gone, Longarm turned to his prisoner and said, "You know what's goin' on, Del. There's a bounty on you, an' I want to get you to Denver safe and whole. In order to do that, I'm gonna need you to give me your promise. I need your promise that you won't try and get away." He chuckled. "Nor shoot me in the back neither. Will you do that?"

"I give you my solemn word, Longarm. Is there a Bible around? Do you want me to swear on one?"

"No, I figure a man who would break his word would

break his pledge just as quick. It's enough for you to tell it to me."

"Well I do," Schrank said.

Half an hour later he had possession of a Smith & Wesson .44 and a gunbelt to go with it.

"I'm not sayin' you'll need that," Longarm said, "but it's better to have a gun an' not need it than to need one an' not have it."

"I appreciate you trusting me with it," Schrank told him.

"All I want is to get you safe to Denver. You can have your say in court and then go on about your life free and clear." He hesitated. "But first we gotta get you safe to Denver."

Chapter 36

Longarm stood at the window of Tim Brightson's town marshal's office. He took a cheroot out and looked it over. He needed to replenish his supply of the smokes. Better do that before heading out toward Wansley, he reminded himself. Good cigars could be hard to find in small towns. Not that Grand Island was any great metropolis, but it was damn sure bigger than any of the burgs farther north.

He turned his head toward Brightson, who was at his desk going over some papers. "Any strangers in town, Tim?"

Brightson looked up, hesitated for a moment, and then laughed. "Longarm, this is a railroad town. Of course there's strangers in town. All day long every day of the week we got strangers in town."

"You're right. Dumb question," Longarm said.

"Apology accepted. What is it you're worried about? That bounty?"

Longarm nodded. He lighted his cheroot and turned to face the town marshal. "I got a responsibility. I don't want to abandon the cat, but I'd rather do that than jeopardize Del Schrank's life."

"You kind of like Schrank, don't you?"

"Yeah, Tim, I suppose I kinda do. When I first seen him I expected him to be stupid. I mean, hell, the man *looks* stupid."

"But he isn't?"

"I'm not so sure," Longarm admitted. "I kinda don't think so. Not no more, I don't."

"Just hope he's smart enough to stick with you instead of trying to run. Coffee?"

Longarm grinned. "Man, I already slosh when I walk."

"Yeah, but do you want some more coffee?"

"Sure, Tim, that sounds like exactly what I need."

Brightson stood and came around his desk to the rusting iron stove on the opposite wall. He carried the well-used coffeepot to Longarm and filled his cup, then went back to his desk to fill his own before returning the pot to the stove. "When do you figure Schrank will be well enough to travel?" he asked.

"Your doc says I maybe could move him tomorrow. The day after that for sure."

"You said you'll need a wagon to carry you up to Wansley?"

"A buckboard would be enough, but any sort of light wagon would do."

"How's about a buggy?"

"Sure, if there's a luggage deck in back."

"I happen to own a buggy. It isn't grand but it's decent."

Longarm raised an eyebrow.

"I know, I know. What the hell is a town marshal, and a city boy at that, doing with a buggy. I won the contraption in a poker game."

"Do you have a horse to go with it?"

"No, but Ben Whitsell at the livery has several that are good driving animals. I can get one of them for you. That way no one will know that you and Schrank are driving up there." He snickered. "You and Schrank and your pussy, that is."

Longarm plucked a dead bug off the windowsill and flung it at the lawman, who was laughing when he ducked.

Chapter 37

"There's an old saying about just this sort of thing," Longarm mused.

"And what might that be?" Schrank asked.

"Beggars can't be choosers."

"Yes," Schrank said, "I see what you mean."

Brightson's buggy was . . . not beautiful. The question was, could it hold together long enough to get them to Wansley? The wheel spokes had splinters protruding as thick as a hard man's beard. The top leather was cracked and torn and the stitching rotted. One side of the seat was held in place with wraps of barbed wire. And there was a gaping hole in the floorboards on the same side as the barbed wire repair.

"I sure hope your marshal friend didn't have more than a dollar in the pot to win this thing."

"Yeah, but at least the horse is a beauty," Longarm said sarcastically. Schrank rolled his eyes. The gelding standing hipshot between the buggy poles was a scrawny, flea-bitten nag, buckskin in color and spooky of nature. It chuffed and stamped a forefoot whenever anyone approached it.

"We might," Longarm said, "be better off to butcher that horse and jerk the meat. What little there'd be of it. You can pull the buggy for us."

"I'd rather hitch the cat and let it pull."

"No," Longarm said judiciously, "the harness is too big."

"There is that." Schrank climbed gingerly into the passenger seat and sat waiting for Longarm to join him.

"One second," Longarm said. "I'll be right back." He stepped out of the livery stable and disappeared onto the street. Several minutes later he was back.

"I got you a present," he said, handing Schrank a rather beat-up and battered double-barrel shotgun with the barrels cut down to twelve or fourteen inches. He gave his prisoner the scattergun and a bag containing several dozen 10-gauge goose loads.

"Think this thing is safe to shoot?"

"From which end," Longarm answered.

Schrank grinned and placed the scattergun across his lap. "Ready if you are."

Longarm took up the driving lines and backed the buckskin out of the central alley in the livery. He took a look up and down the street, but if anyone was interested in their early morning departure, they were not obvious about it.

He clucked to the horse, and they began to roll north, away from the railroad tracks.

The cat, in its cage strapped on the luggage shelf, began to hiss and spit when the buggy wheels jarred across the ruts. Schrank turned around, but Longarm ignored the beast. He and that cat were simply not fond of one another.

He figured by the time they reached Wansley, the damn thing would either have gotten used to the ride or it would have shaken its guts loose. Either would be all right with him.

Chapter 38

"Did you remember to bring something for us to eat?" Schrank asked.

"Always prepared, that's my motto," Longarm said as he shook the driving lines to lengthen the buckskin's stride just a little.

"So can we stop, please? I'm over here considering starvation as my next pastime."

Longarm looked over at his prisoner, then over his shoulder through the isinglass back window. "When we find a good place to stop."

"A good place? Shit, man, just stop anyplace along here. These farmers won't mind. It isn't like we're going to leave a mess or anything. Come to that, I'll clean up behind us my own self."

"It isn't that," Longarm said, shaking his head.

"What then?"

"I take it you haven't been paying no mind to whoever is back there following us."

"Fo— Oh, shit." Schrank turned around in his seat and tried to look out to the slightly distorted view seen through the thin sheet of mica, gave up, and hung out the side of the buggy to stare behind them.

Longarm reached out and grabbed him by the arm, yanking him back upright on the padded seat.

"What the . . . ?"

"You want t'look out the window, that's fine. They aren't likely to notice from that far back, but if you try to ride outside the damn buggy, somebody's sure t'see. I don't want that. Don't want them to know that we know they're back there."

"What do you think . . . Ah, never mind. I know good and well why somebody would be following us. A thousand dollars, that's why."

Longarm grunted his affirmation of the comment.

"So what do we do now?" Schrank asked.

The response was a grin that held no mirth in it but did cause one side of Longarm's mustache to rise. "Why, Del lad, we stop an' have us some lunch, that's what."

Chapter 39

"Perfect," Longarm said as the buggy rattled and shook down a rock-strewn slope and splashed across a slow-moving rill. The hooves of the buckskin frightened a school of under-sized pan fish, bluegills perhaps. It was only a guess. Longarm did not know the names of any other species of small pan fish and cared less.

Schrank peered down into the water, which was quickly muddied by the passage of the buggy's wheels. "Surely you aren't thinking to stop and fish for our lunch," he said.

"No, I got something else in mind." Longarm's smile was grim as he encouraged the scrawny horse up the other side.

"Mind if I ask . . . Here? We're going to stop here for lunch?" Schrank sounded worried.

"I thought you were the lad who for the last three miles has been complaining how hungry he is," Longarm said, as he guided the buckskin off the road and into the thicket of trees that lined both sides of the waterway. But not very far off the road and not into the most dense part of the thicket.

"I think I lost my appetite," Schrank groaned.

Longarm laughed out loud. And brought the buggy to a halt with its rear—and the cat cage—facing back the way they had just come. He hopped down from the rickety driving box, hooked the hitch weight to the horse's bit, and fetched a feed bag from beneath the seat. The bag was heavy with a half gallon of mixed corn and oats he'd bought back at the livery. With a little bit of finagling he was able to fit the bag over bit and lead so the horse would be held in place but could still eat.

"You can get out now if you like," he said.

"And if I don't like?"

Longarm shrugged. "Stay there if you'd rather. It don't make no nevermind to me."

Schrank got out of the buggy. But his expression made it clear he did not really like the idea.

"What I'd like you to do," Longarm said, "is to set right there." He pointed to a spot near the right front wheel of the buggy.

"Sit there and do what exactly?"

Longarm's grin flashed. "Why, I expect you to have your lunch, of course. Go on. Set down now." He took the shotgun from Schrank and placed it on the buggy seat, then retrieved a cloth sack from beneath the seat. The bag held some jerky, cold biscuits, and a folded scrap of oilcloth containing ready-ground coffee.

"You got any matches?" he asked.

Schrank nodded.

"Then why don't you make us a fire so's we can boil up a little coffee after we eat."

"You got a coffeepot in that bag?"

"Got a gallon-size tin can."

"That should do."

"Get us some water from the crick, will you."

"What about you?"

Longarm slid the shotgun off the buggy seat and transferred into his right-hand coat pocket a handful of shotgun shells from the bag Tim Brightson had given him. He was wishing as he did so that he had thought to borrow a rifle from Brightson too, but it was a little late for that now.

"Oh," Schrank said. "I, um, see what you have in mind."

"Make plenty of smoke," Longarm suggested, "and if you feel like talking to yourself, that'd be fine too. An' don't worry if I happen t'be gone for a spell."

He scrambled down the slope to the creek and waded across it, his eyes already searching ahead for a good spot close to the road where he could lie in ambush.

Behind him Del Schrank and the buckskin horse were having a loud—if one-sided—conversation about treachery and fair-weather friends.

Chapter 40

Longarm's lips pulled back into a ghost of a grin . . . although no one who saw it could ever have mistaken it for a pleasant expression.

The horsemen were approaching the crossing. Three of them. Armed with handguns only. He did not see a carbine or a shotgun in the bunch.

They looked like a bunch of saloon layabouts. Probably if they ever got their hands on a thousand dollars—and Longarm was quite certain they were not going to do so by claiming the bounty on Del Schrank's head—they would not be able to figure out how to divide it three ways. Assholes, he thought, and that was being charitable.

The fellow in the lead had reddish blond hair. He needed a haircut and a shave. A new shirt too, as his ancient red garment looked like he had been wearing it, without bothering to wash it, since Methuselah was a pup. His gun leather looked like it had been cared for though, and that suggested that his revolver was clean and in good condition as well.

Asshole number two had on a greasy, grimy derby hat and a small revolver of some sort carried in a shoulder rig under his left armpit. Anyone who wore a pistol in that fashion had to be either very, very good with it . . . or not know a pistol from a piss.

The third member of this hunting party was plump and clean-shaven. He bounced with every step his horse took. A city boy talked into coming along with his drinking buddies, Longarm suspected. He had a revolver strapped on but likely did not know how to use it worth a damn.

So the order of events was easy to calculate. Shoot Blondie first, Derby second, and shout boo at the third idiot to frighten him away like a hant on All Hallow's Eve.

They were halfway down the slope leading to the water before the idiots ever saw, or maybe heard, Del and the horse chattering away on the other side of the creek. They drew rein in great surprise and turned to go back up onto level ground.

There they dismounted and had a powwow, then the first two handed their reins to Fat Boy, took their revolvers in hand, and set off a-hunting they to go.

It might have been funny if it hadn't been Longarm and Del Schrank they were hunting.

Longarm watched with some amusement as instead of simply walking across the ford, they dropped into a low crouch and began what they seemed to believe was a sneak through the woods.

Carefully and as silently as he could, Longarm eared back both hammers on the sawed-off 10-gauge and waited for company to arrive. Just in time for dinner too.

Chapter 41

The idea was simple enough. Drop tough-looking Blondie with the first shot, swing the barrels left quickly, and use the remaining shell to take down Derby, then out with the Colt and shoot Fat Boy ... if he was still in the game at that point. Longarm rather suspected that a soft-looking fellow like Fat Boy would be on his knees blubbering for mercy once he saw his companions with their guts spread out on the ground.

Longarm waited until the would-be shooters were perhaps twenty feet away, then rose to his knees and called out, "Hold it right there. You're under arrest."

It was a stupid thing to have to say, he agreed, but it was what they were supposed to do before they took somebody down.

Not that he had any idea what he was supposed to be arresting them for, as they had not broken any laws. Yet. Even a complete idiot of a lawyer could point out that all they had really done to this point was to stop their horses beside a public roadway and walk away a few feet.

They could—that is, *could*—intend to take a piss. With

their guns in hand. Perhaps they had to take a piss *and* were deathly afraid of snakes. Longarm knew better. Anyone with half a grain of sense would know better. But a lawyer would argue it anyway, and a judge would almost certainly dismiss the charges and turn them loose.

If—that is, *if*—they did not accomplish their thousand-dollar purpose and kill both Custis Long and Delbert Schrank first.

Still, the law was supposed to be observed on the subject, so he called loud and clear, "Hold it right there. You're under arrest."

The results were predictable.

Blondie dropped into a crouch and took aim with his Smith & Wesson.

Derby stood where he was looking slightly confused and searching for something to shoot at. He obviously had not seen Longarm's ambush.

Fat Boy did not seem to know that anything was happening. But then he was some feet away and might not have heard.

Longarm already had the shotgun pointed at Blondie's belly. He pulled the front trigger.

Both hammers dropped at the same time, sending a torrent of lead and flame out of the front of those truncated barrels and damned near dislocating Longarm's right shoulder. As it was, the recoil pushed him back two or three feet and made him wish he had taken up some other line of work.

The results were not so bad though. Blondie simply ceased to exist as two entire 10-gauge loads ripped through his belly and came out behind him in a spray of scarlet. His right arm, which had been extended with the Smith in hand, was stripped of flesh and muscle so there was little left but shattered bone, while his revolver was thrown back and up where it caromed off his face like a billiard ball driving hard off a side rail.

The bloody pile of offal that seconds before had been a living, breathing human wound up crumpled onto the roadside.

And Custis Long wound up holding a smoking—but now empty—scattergun in his hands.

Derby was not so encumbered. The man had not been prepared for Longarm's challenge, but he responded to it almost as quickly as Blondie had.

His undersized, nickel-plated revolver spat immediately, pointing in the general direction of the cloud of white powder smoke left by the discharge of those two 10-gauge shells.

Longarm did not know where Derby's first bullet went. It was not close enough for him to hear. Or possibly he was so deafened by the roar of those shotgun blasts that he simply could not hear the bullet's passage. In either case the wildly fired shot did not connect, giving Longarm time to drop the damn misfiring shotgun and palm his .45.

"Drop it," he shouted. "You're under arrest, dammit." And this time he had cause to arrest the son of a bitch. Assault on a federal officer was reason enough to bring them all in.

At least he *thought* he shouted. He opened his mouth and formed the words, but he could hear nothing except a dull emptiness in his ears.

Whether sound came out or not, Derby made no effort to comply. Instead he found his point of aim. Which was right down Custis Long's throat.

Longarm shot the man square in the chest before he could get the next round off, then he aimed carefully and shot him again, this time in the face.

Derby's derby came flying off and sailed to the ground a good ten feet behind where the man had been standing.

"Had" been because he dropped like a poleaxed steer and hit the ground well before his hat did.

Longarm sighed and stood upright. These two bounty hunters would not earn their reward. Not the kind they had intended anyway, although it could be said that they had indeed gone to their reward. Such as it was.

He straightened his shoulders and shoved the Colt back into its leather.

There was just one thing he had forgotten.

Fat Boy, who'd looked so lost and hopeless, had more balls than Longarm had given him credit for.

The third bounty hunter was no gunman—no surprise there—but either he wanted to take prisoners or avenge his fallen comrades or some damn thing. For whatever reason, Fat Boy ducked his head, balled his fists, and came charging full speed toward Longarm with the obvious intention of battering him into the ground.

"Oh, shit," Longarm muttered.

Chapter 42

Fat Boy ran square into a face full of fist. The man's lips split and his nose pulped and there was gore running off all the rolls of his chin and down onto a neck that looked like it belonged on a good-sized bull calf.

Longarm stepped back and waited for him to fall.

He didn't. Instead he tucked his head down lower onto that thick neck and came on again.

Longarm hit him again.

This time he fell. And bounced back up like he was an India rubber ball.

"You son of a bitch," Fat Boy cried.

Longarm was pleased. His hearing seemed to be coming back a little.

Fat Boy attacked again. He was, if nothing else, a persistent pup, Longarm thought. Another punch in the face filled the air with splattered blood and possibly a tooth or two.

Fat Boy went down. Got up. Was knocked down again.

"Dammit, man," Longarm yelped. "Stay down, will you?"

"Murderer," Fat Boy shrieked.

Longarm's hearing was definitely returning. Or Fat Boy was god-awful loud.

Longarm had no idea how long their one-sided dance might have gone on except for Del Schrank. Schrank waded across the ford, came up behind Fat Boy, and conked him over the head with the butt of the revolver Longarm had given him.

This time Fat Boy stayed down.

Chapter 43

"Get these things off'n me! I know my rights. I am a member of a posse comitatus and you got no authority on me." Fat Boy looked quite peeved to find himself cuffed to a back wheel of Tim Brightson's buggy.

"Posse comitatus, eh?" Longarm said. "So who's the sheriff that swore you in?"

"It wasn't a sheriff," Fat Boy snapped back at him. "It was me and Tom and George. We formed our own posse."

"Going to collect a big reward, were you?"

"That's right. A thousand dollars. George said so."

"Let me guess. George was the fella in front of that little charge," Longarm said.

"That's right. George Stein. He and Tom Watkin formed the posse and invited me to join them. All's I had to do was look after the horses and get a hundred dollars for it."

"While they split the nine hundred." Longarm shook his head. "Some friends you got, uh . . . Come to think of it, what is your name?"

"I am Ronald K. Jellicoe. Now, take these handcuffs off me."

"First, you do know that I killed your friends, don't you?" Longarm asked.

"I know it, and believe me, you will pay for it." Jellicoe lifted his chin and glared first at Longarm and then at Del Schrank, who was tending the coffeepot and the little fire it sat above.

"Let me introduce myself," Longarm said. He produced his wallet with the badge in it. "Deputy United States Marshal Custis Long," he said, "an' those are my handcuffs you're wearing."

"But I have done nothing wrong. I was completely within my rights as a member of a posse comi—"

"Yeah, right, posse comitatus. You said that already. What you don't seem to know is that your posse, such as it was, wasn't legal. A posse has to be got together by what they call competent legal authority. Which I am sure neither George nor . . . What was that other one, Dan? Don?"

"Tom," Jellicoe said. "His name was Tom Watkin."

"Yeah. Him. Well, your buddies George an' Tom didn't have no authority to raise a posse. Worse, when the three o' you tried to kill me, what you done was to assault a federal officer. That right there is a prison offense, Ronnie-boy." Longarm gave Fat Boy a grin that held not a shred of mirth. "What you done, Ronnie, is to step in shit up to your ears." He turned his head. "Is that coffee ready, Del?"

"Just about."

"Just about is good enough. Let me have some."

"We only have the one cup," Schrank said.

"You and me can share it. Ronnie don't need any."

"Hey, that isn't fair!"

Longarm looked down at Jellicoe, who was sitting on the ground beside the wheel, and said, "Haven't you heard? Life ain't fair. Now, shut your mouth and act nice. The law says I have to feed you twice a day, but it doesn't say that I got to feed you good. You'll get a drink o' water now and maybe something to eat tonight."

He shifted his attention and said to Schrank, "We'll load those bodies onto their horses an' turn loose of 'em to go back home on their own."

"What about his horse?" Schrank asked, hooking a thumb in the direction of Ronald K. Jellicoe.

"We'll chain him through the cantle to keep him on the saddle whether he wants to or not, then tie the horse to the back o' the buggy. And while I think about it, Del, please check the saddlebags on all three horses. We'll take whatever food an' coffee they got. Then let's be on our way. We already lost more'n enough time here."

Schrank gave Jellicoe a look of pure disgust. "Figured to take me back dead so you could collect that reward, did you?"

"I . . ." Jellicoe shivered and looked away, unable to meet Schrank's eyes any longer.

Longarm took the buckskin out from between the poles and led it down to the creek so it could drink while Schrank tended to the other animals.

A thousand dollars, Longarm grumbled to himself. Who the hell knew what lay ahead with that much money on their heads?

Chapter 44

Wansley was . . . not very damn much. What there was, however, was surprising.

In addition to several dozen houses there was a farm supply store, a post office, and—the surprising thing, at least to Longarm—a chicken hatchery, right out there in the middle of nowhere.

Longarm handed the driving lines to Del Schrank and said, "I'll go inside and see where it is we're supposed to deliver this damn cat."

"We'll be here when you get back," Schrank assured him.

Longarm waited until he was on the stoop in front of the farm supply before he looked back and with a wink said, "If the fat boy gives you any trouble, Del, you can shoot him. I'll write down 'attempting to escape' on my report."

"Hey!" Jellicoe yelped.

"Then shut up and mind your manners," Longarm advised, and then he went inside the store.

"How can I help you, mister?"

"I'm looking for the owner of a cat I got outside."

"Really? Oh, the ladies have been in here looking for

you every day, sometimes two or three times. They will be mighty happy to see you."

"No happier'n I will be to get rid of that critter. Can you tell me how to find them?"

"That's easy enough." The storekeeper pointed. "You go three houses past the hatchery, then one over. You're looking for Edna Cantwell."

"I thought I was looking for . . ."

"Cleo Isaacson. That's right. She owns Sam, but she is staying with Mrs. Cantwell. It is Mrs. Cantwell's house I directed you to."

"Lord, mister, you know the cat's name an' everything?"

The man grinned. " 'Everything' is just about right. We all know pretty much everything about each other around here."

Longarm thanked the man and started toward the door but stopped and turned back. "Mind if I ask you something?"

"Anything."

"How's come you have a bird hatchery out here so far from everything?"

"It's a new venture that seems to be catching on. The Montgomery Ward Company contracted with Wansley Hatchery to breed chickens and deliver them by mail. Naturally the chicks have to be hatched close to their market to make sure they don't die in transit, so the contract hatcheries are scattered all over. Nebraska is growing when it comes to farming and small ranch holdings, and they decided to do business with our hatchery."

"They deliver chicks, not chickens?"

"That's right. Four different breeds so far."

"But how . . .?"

The storekeeper laughed. "By mail, of course. You wouldn't think it to look at our village, but our post office is one of the busiest in the state. We're all quite proud of Wansley Hatchery."

"An' you should be." Longarm touched the brim of his Stetson and went back outside, to find Schrank amusing himself by giving evil looks to Jellicoe.

"Move over, Del. We know where we're goin' now."

Chapter 45

"Sam!" the girl's shriek could probably be heard all the way over in Omaha. Maybe in Julesburg in the other direction.

For the first time in a very long while, Longarm was caught flat-footed. He expected any pal of Mrs. Vail to be in her sixties at the very least or possibly older. This girl was a beauty. Probably in her early thirties, with chestnut brown hair done up in rolls—there was a name for that, but at the moment Longarm could not recall what it might be—and a buxom figure. She was wearing a housecoat that had been washed until it was paper thin. Just a little bit thinner would have been even better as far as Longarm was concerned.

Longarm and Del Schrank stood on the porch looking useless—which at the moment they indeed were—while the chestnut-haired beauty finished shouting. Which she did as soon as she was joined by two other women, both of them graying but dignified and, he would guess, in their sixties or seventies.

"Excuse me." The girl had dimples when she smiled. Seeing them made Longarm want to send up some Chinese exploding rockets. "Sir? Excuse me, sir?" She had to take him by the coat sleeve to get his attention. All he wanted to do at the moment was stare at her.

Longarm grabbed his Stetson and held it down by his belt buckles. "Yes, miss?"

"May we know your names?"

"Oh, uh, yes'm." Longarm quickly introduced Schrank—without mentioning that he was a prisoner—and then himself.

"This is Mrs. Isaacson," she said, motioning, "and this is my mother, Mrs. Cantwell."

Longarm made a leg and gave the ladies his very best smile. "A pleasure, I'm sure." He looked at the daughter, who said, "I am Trudy Dillard."

"Is that short for Gertrude, Miss Dillard?"

"It is Mrs. Dillard, and Trudy is my given name."

"Sorry, Miz Dillard."

Trudy shifted back a few inches to where neither her mother nor Mrs. Isaacson could see. She batted her eyes quite suggestively and added, "I am a widow, Mr. Long."

"Sorry t'hear that, ma'am." He wasn't, but it was the right thing to say.

The ladies had freed Sam from his confinement, and now the fool thing was crawling all over Mrs. Isaacson and purring loud enough for Longarm to hear over the clucking and fussing going on inside the hatchery. The hissing, spitting, howling monster had been reduced to being a baby doll.

"Did my darling Sammie give you any trouble, Mr. Long?"

"No, ma'am." That was a bald-faced lie, but what the hell. They were here now and the damn cat was off his hands. Finally.

"He is such a good boy," the lady cooed. "Aren't you, precious."

Longarm thought he might puke. He managed to keep everything down. Barely.

"Would you gentlemen care for . . ."

"Longarm!" Schrank's shout of warning came a split second before the sound of a weapon discharging.

Chapter 46

The stupid, bounty-hunting son of a bitch was across the street standing behind a thick cloud of white smoke. He held a single-shot carbine of some sort and was intent on trying to reload it as he did not seem to have a handgun, at least none that Longarm could see from where he stood.

"Stay here," Longarm ordered Del Schrank as he leaped off the porch and charged straight at the shooter, .45 in hand and blood in his eye.

The shooter saw him coming and turned and fled, running out into the street and toward the hatchery.

Longarm pounded after him. He shouted the obligatory "stop or I'll shoot" warning.

The shooter was a tall, lanky kid with tousled yellow hair and bib overalls. He was also fast as hell, and for a moment Longarm thought the fellow might get away.

Longarm snapped a shot in his direction, more to get his attention, and perhaps scare him into giving himself up, than in any hope of hitting anything. To make sure he did not hit some innocent bystander, he aimed deliberately high.

Instead of convincing the fellow to surrender, it only spurred him to greater exertion. And speed.

The shooter bolted through the front door of the Wansley Hatchery and disappeared inside.

Longarm growled unhappily. If the fellow had time enough to stop and reload, he would have the advantage when it came to firepower.

No one wants to barrel full-tilt through a doorway when there is likely to be someone on the other side with a high-powered carbine waiting to put a heavy bullet through one's chest.

Still, it was something that had to be done. Longarm threw himself full speed through the hatchery doorway and into the gloom and stink of the interior. He damn near gagged at the heavy ammonia smell of chicken droppings.

The birds were everywhere. Straw-filled nests lined the walls on either side. Round tin feeders were placed every ten feet or so, and there were water tubs between the feeders.

The floor was covered with a carpet of gray-and-white speckled birds that squawked and flapped and set up a din that was as harsh on the ears as their shit was harsh in the nose.

Longarm's focus was not on the stupid birds, however, but on the shooter who . . . There! The SOB was on the far side of the long, narrow hatchery floor, crouching more or less behind one of the feeders.

Off to one side a pair of very startled hatchery workers stood gaping at this sudden intrusion.

"Surrender yourself," Longarm shouted. It was doubtful the man could hear over the din of the clucking birds.

The shooter had taken up the wrong profession.

Not that he was a professional when it came to murder. Far from it. The poor sap seemed to barely know how to shoot, much less how to kill an armed man.

He lifted his carbine and raised up a little so he could see over the top of the feeder. He took aim at Longarm and bent to line up his sights.

He had no more time left.

Longarm had little choice but to put the man down.

Longarm's .45 roared. Smoke and flame spat out of the muzzle of his Colt, and at the other end of the hatchery a heavy slug sent the bounty hunter flying backward into the slimy bird shit that covered the floor. His carbine discharged into the ceiling and the weapon flew out of his hands.

The din of the chickens before had been nothing compared with the explosion of noise that filled the place in response to the gunfire. Panicked birds flew up and scattered in all directions as they tried blindly to get away. All the birds that had covered the floor now filled the air. The fool creatures bumped into each other and tumbled to the floor, only to jump up and try to fly away again. Dust and feathers were so thick in the air it was difficult to breathe. Longarm must have been crashed into a dozen times in as many seconds. He stood with his Colt poised in hand but with no chance he could see to the far end of the hatchery, because of all the flapping, fluttering birds that were in the way.

After what seemed like a terribly long time but probably was not, he saw someone approaching. The Colt was not needed, though. The newcomer wore a filthy linen duster covering his clothing and knee-high rubber boots on his feet. He had a cotton mask tied over his mouth and nose, but Longarm had no fear that the mask was intended to hide identity. Rather it was an aid to breathing inside the heavy stink of the hatchery.

"Are you all right, mister?" the man asked.

"I am, but what about him?"

Longarm walked with the hatchery worker—carefully because the floor was slippery with feathers, straw, and chicken droppings—to the far end of the building, where the other employee was kneeling beside the body of the would-be bounty hunter.

The shooter was dead. A battered old Sharps single-shot carbine lay several feet away, where it had flown from his dying hands.

"Mister, uh . . ."

Longarm identified himself, and the workers visibly relaxed.

"D'you know him?" Longarm asked.

The two men could only shrug and shake their heads.

"It don't matter, I suppose. Well look, uh, do you have an undertaker here?"

"Mister, we got eggs. We got about five tons of cracked grain. We don't even got a saloon, much less a marshal or a buryin' man."

"You got a shovel?"

"Yes, of course we got shovels."

"Then bury this son of a bitch before your chickens start to eat the poor dead bastard." Longarm turned on his heel and left, heading back to make sure Del Schrank was all right.

Schrank was, but Mrs. Dillard was not.

He found Schrank and the older ladies gathered in horror on the porch beside the blood-covered figure of the pretty lady with the chestnut hair.

Longarm raced up onto the porch and knelt.

This, then, was where the shooter's errant bullet had flown.

"Get the doctor," he ordered. "Quick."

Chapter 47

"We don't have a doctor," Mrs. Cantwell wailed. "The nearest one is forty miles away."

"A vet then," Longarm said quickly.

The woman gave him an odd look. "An old soldier?"

"No, you . . ." Longarm bit back the retort he wanted to make. "No, ma'am. A veterinarian. A horse doctor. Surely you have one of those."

"No, we don't. We don't have . . . Oh, God, Trudy is going to die, isn't she?"

"Let's hope not," Longarm said. He looked up at Schrank, who was hovering nearby and looking about half-sick. "Help me carry her, Del. We need to get her onto a bed someplace where she can be looked at." To the ladies he said, "Show me where we can put her."

"In her bed, I think," Mrs. Cantwell said.

"Del, get on that side. Help me pick her up. Ma'am, show us where to take her."

"This way."

Mrs. Isaacson held the door as wide as it would go while Del Schrank knelt beside Mrs. Dillard opposite Longarm. As gently as they could, Longarm and Schrank picked up the injured woman and carried her along behind her mother.

"In here." The room was frilly, a study in chintz and flowered wallpaper. Longarm did not really know about such things but it struck him as a room that might belong to a girl instead of a widow. Likely it was not much changed from when the wounded lady had been Trudy Cantwell.

The two men placed the patient onto her bed but not before her mother rushed to put some towels down in an attempt to keep blood from getting onto the bedding. As soon as Mrs. Dillard was settled, Schrank made an escape from the room.

"Get me some bandages an' a basin of water," Longarm said. "And I want at least one of you to be here inside this room all the time. I'm gonna have to cut some of her clothes off and I don't want you to think that I ... um ... Just stay in the room with her, please."

The blood seemed to be coming from high on her left side, close to her armpit. He could see that she had been wounded in the upper left arm as well. There was only the one bullet, so likely it had passed between her arm and upper body. That right there made him suspect that the wound was not life- threatening. Bloody and painful, but not a death sentence, not if it did not turn septic. Gangrene in a place that could not be cut off was sure and certain death.

Rather than have Mrs. Cantwell fumble around looking for scissors, Longarm took out his pocket knife and used it to cut Mrs. Dillard's clothing away from her upper body.

Mrs. Cantwell gave him some towels that he used to mop away blood so he could see what he was dealing with.

The bullet seemed to have cut across the skin beside Mrs. Dillard's left breast—a rather shapely breast, he could not help but notice—probably breaking a rib at the same time.

The inside of her left arm was more scraped than anything but deeply enough to cause some bleeding.

Once Longarm cleaned up the blood there, it seeped rather than flowed. He tied a bandage around her arm and figured that would be enough. It was a different story on her upper body, where a four-inch-long ragged slice continued to bleed.

He applied pressure, which seemed to slow the bleeding. It should stop it soon, he thought.

Damn, that was one fine-looking tit. It was hard not to stare, and after a few moments the lady's mother came over and placed another towel over her torso so Longarm could no longer see the pale and lovely breast.

"You got some carbolic acid?" he asked.

"What is that?"

"Never mind. How 'bout clean water?"

Mrs. Cantwell sniffed. "Well, of course we have that, young man."

"Let me have a basin of it, please."

Once he had the water, he used it to clean away the dried blood that he could reach, while continuing to put pressure over the wound. The bleeding slowed, and after what seemed a long time but probably was not more than ten minutes, the flow ceased.

Longarm grunted his satisfaction and took the bloody cloth away. "I want you to wrap her, uh, chest with bandages. She shouldn't likely start to bleed, but if she does, call me. Mostly I'm concerned about her ribs. I think one of 'em is busted, so wrap her kinda tight." He looked down at Mrs. Dillard, who was peering silently up at him, as she had been throughout. "This will hurt, ma'am, but it's gotta be done."

"I trust you," she whispered.

Longarm smiled at her.

"Mama," she called to her mother.

"Yes, dear?"

"Have Mr . . . I'm sorry, I've forgotten your name."

"Long, miss."

She looked at her mother and said, "Please have Mr. Long and his friend stay over. If I start bleeding again or . . . anything . . . I would like to have him near. Give the gentlemen a good supper and let them stay in Donny's room."

"All right, dear." To Longarm the lady explained, "Don is my son, Trudy's brother."

"Yes, ma'am."

"Mr. Long, I would feel better about all this if you would look in on me every so often."

"I'd be glad t'do that, ma'am."

Mrs. Dillard closed her eyes. "I'm a little tired now, Mama. I'll sleep for a bit. then maybe, Mama, you could fix me some nice chicken broth."

"Of course, dear. Anything you like."

At least, Longarm thought, they won't have any trouble coming up with a chicken to stew for the broth. There looked to be ten thousand or more of the creatures just down the way at the Wansley Hatchery.

Longarm turned and tiptoed out to the porch, where he found Del Schrank.

"We're stayin' the night here," he said.

Schrank nodded. "What are we going to do with Ronald K. Jellicoe there?"

Jellicoe was still chained to the saddle of his horse, and it was secured to the back of Tim Brightson's borrowed buggy.

"Shit!" Longarm said. "I forgot about him complete. I guess we'll . . . I dunno. Fasten him round a tree or something until tomorrow. Reckon we'll take him back to Denver with us so's he can stand trial in federal court there. Bastard sure is a nuisance though."

"You could let him go," Schrank suggested.

Longarm raised an eyebrow. "He was tryin' to kill you, y'know."

Schrank shrugged. "But he didn't. Go ahead. Let him loose."

"If that's what you want to do, it don't make no nevermind to me. After all, him and his pals already came out on the short end o' things."

"Go ahead then."

"All right, if you say so."

"I do. Really."

Longarm left the Cantwell porch and strode out to the street where the buggy was parked. He paused to light a cheroot, then said, "This is your lucky day, Jellicoe."

He unlocked the handcuffs and removed them, then took the reins of the prisoner's horse and handed them to the fat man.

"Get outta my sight. But mind that if I see you again, I'll kill you. Now, go."

The words had barely left Longarm's lips before Jellicoe wheeled his horse around and put his heels to the animal.

Longarm yawned and went back to the Cantwell porch to sit and wait for supper.

Chapter 48

After the ladies went to bed, Longarm took the liberty of drawing a pitcher of hot water from the reservoir on the side of the kitchen range. He took it back to the room where he and Schrank were sharing a bed, poured it into the blue and white bedside basin, and treated himself to a thorough sponge bath. The evidence given by his nose suggested the washing was much overdue.

When he was clean again, he pulled a pair of cotton drawers out of his carpetbag and slipped those on. They felt damn good after the sweaty, clammy balbriggans he had been wearing for much too long.

"Is there any hot water left over?" Schrank asked.

"Dunno if it's hot, but it'd be at least warm."

"You done with it?"

"I am. You're welcome to the rest, Del. Want me to go draw you some more?"

"No, I won't need much." Schrank opened the bedroom window and tossed out the water in the basin that Longarm had used.

Longarm spotted a red and black striped Mexican poncho
hanging on a peg, likely belonging to Trudy's brother Don.
Rather than get completely dressed again he pulled the poncho over his head.

"Where are you off to at this time of night?"

"Thought I'd go check on our patient. I promised I'd look
in on her from time to time."

Schrank grinned. "You just want to get another look at her
tits."

"Certainly not!" Longarm retorted. But he could not sup-
press a smile. "On t'other hand, I reckon I could stand it if
she could."

"Just don't wake me when you get back."

Longarm eased barefoot out into the hallway and went
silently to the next doorway, which was Trudy's. A lamp
burned softly, the wick turned down low, on the bedside
table.

Mrs. Dillard appeared to be asleep. Longarm turned the
wick up until he could see, then gently pulled the sheet
down.

A frilly nightdress covered her to her toes, so in order to
check the progress of the wounds he had no choice but to
raise the hem of the nightdress all the way to her chin.

The ladies seemed to have done a good job bandaging
Trudy. The strips of cloth wound over her breasts and around
her chest were very lightly spotted with some seepage of
blood, but the bleeding had stopped by now and her breathing was slow and steady.

Longarm could not help but glance at the patch of dark
pubic hair that lay curly in the lamplight.

He looked Trudy over from her toes, up a pair of very
shapely legs, past those curls, and on to the splash of stark
white bandage.

Her hair was loose now and spread across the pillow.

Her eyes were shiny and bright, reflecting the light from the lamp flame.

Longarm blinked.

Trudy's eyes were wide open. She was looking back at him. When his eyes locked with hers, she smiled. "What time is it?"

Longarm shrugged. "I dunno. Late."

"Are you married?"

It seemed an odd question, but he answered it honestly. "No, ma'am, I ain't."

"Ma'am? Do I look like a 'ma'am' to you?"

"What you look like to me is somethin' I oughtn't to be sayin' in polite company."

"It could be I'm not as polite as you might think. Not as fragile either."

"But you . . ."

"I am a widowed lady, Marshal Long. My husband has been dead for three and a half years, and I haven't had a man inside me in all that time. I don't mean to shock you, but I like to . . . do that."

He chuckled. "Can't say as I blame you."

"Any man around here would brag and crow about being the one to nail the Widow Dillard. I know them and I wouldn't trust a one of them. You, on the other hand . . ."

"Won't be around here t'crow even if I was of a mind to," Longarm finished for her.

She smiled. "Exactly."

"But you're hurt. You got a busted rib. I can't crawl on top of—"

"Wait," she said. "Help me roll over onto my right side. Now, you lie down nice and close behind me. You don't have to get naked. Just flip Donny's serape thing out of the way and pull down whatever you're wearing under it. You are wearing something under it, aren't you?"

He laughed. "Yes, I am."

"Then pull them down and come onto this bed. That's right. Nice and close. Like a pair of spoons lying together in the dish drain. Yes, and put your thing . . . *oh*! You are so *big*."

"D'you mind?"

"Mind? Dear man, I love it." As if to demonstrate the truth of that statement, Trudy pushed back against him, hard, driving his cock all the deeper into the sweet heat of her body.

Longarm smiled and allowed her to do the bumping and grinding so he would not hurt her if he got a little too rambunctious in their coupling.

He wouldn't mind spending some time with this girl once she was healed and able to fling her ass without having to hold anything back.

But in the meantime . . . this would certainly do.

Chapter 49

"Don't you look like the cat that ate the canary," Del Schrank said with a grin.

"Huh. I know that cat, an' I wouldn't trust it with a canary nor with anything else. Truth is, I damn near stepped on the sonuvabitch in the hallway. Thought about kicking it but passed up the opportunity."

"You wouldn't think it was the same cat that you hauled here from Denver, would you?" Schrank said.

"I shoulda just turned it loose an' left it there. On the other hand, just think what I woulda missed if I'd done that."

"And just what would you have missed?" Schrank asked, his grin becoming wider.

"No need t'talk about that," Longarm said. "Now, finish getting dressed. Miz Cantwell is waiting breakfast for us. Smells mighty good too."

Longarm stood and stamped his feet into his boots, then pulled on his tweed coat. He already was wearing his Stetson hat and his gunbelt. Those were practically the first things he put on in the morning, right after his britches and his shirt.

"How is your patient?" Schrank asked.

"Tolerable."

"Why, I thought she was near to death, what with all the time you spent in her room last night. Taking good care of her, I'm sure."

"I managed t'pull her back from the precipice."

"Nice precipice."

"The rest of her ain't bad either. Now, shut up an' let's go eat."

An hour later Longarm and Del Schrank had the buggy hitched and were looking back at Wansley through the dust their wheels raised.

Half a day after that they were approaching the creek where Ronald K. Jellicoe and his now dead friends had thought to lay their ambush.

"Del, do you remember us dropping anything, empty tin cans or the like, over on the far side o' that creek when we was here before?"

"No. Why do you ask?"

Longarm drew back on the lines to bring the buggy horse to a halt. "Because I seen the sunlight reflecting off something shiny over there. Metal o' some sort, it looked like."

Schrank shook his head. "I don't know what it could be."

Longarm's expression became grim. "I got an idea. You got a safety thong over the hammer of that hogleg?"

"Of course. I wouldn't want the thing to fall out of the holster."

"Well, slip that thong off an' make sure the gun is loose in the leather. That reflection might not mean anything, but we ain't gonna take any chances."

Longarm put the horse into a slow walk, and while they rolled forward he talked over a few things with Del Schrank.

Chapter 50

As they neared the slope leading down to the creek, Longarm wrapped the lines around the whip socket, careful to
leave a little tension in the reins so there would be some
contact with the bit. Otherwise the buggy horse could be
expected to stop.

"Now?" Schrank asked.

"Now," Longarm agreed.

Schrank slipped down to the ground on his side of the rig
while Longarm did the same on the opposite side of the seat.
The horse continued on, pulling an empty buggy along the
road and down to the rill of running water.

Schrank had the sawed-off shotgun while Longarm
palmed his Colt. Together they dropped into a crouch and
scurried into the woods that lined the little creek.

Longarm heard the splash of hooves as the horse entered
the water. Then he heard a loud "get them, boys" and a rattle
of gunfire. At least three guns, he thought. Maybe four.

A horse whinnied—the buggy horse, he thought—and
the shooting came to an abrupt stop.

"Where the hell are they?"

"Do you see any bodies?"

"I'm sure I shot one of the sons of bitches."

"You idiot, there's nothing in that outfit now but bullet holes."

"Well, then they fell in the damn creek."

"Where could they have got to?"

It was a reasonable question, Longarm thought as he climbed the opposite bank. He was about to give them an answer.

He stopped at the same spot where he had shot it out with Jellicoe and his friends. The view on the road was much the same as it had been then. There were three men gathered around the buggy. Hell, they were making this easy.

Longarm stood and called, "You're all under arrest, you dumb fuckers."

All three spun to face him, guns coming up as they turned. These were not the inexperienced idiots he had faced before, though. This crew knew what gunplay meant.

Longarm shot the tall galoot who looked the most like he knew what he was doing. Longarm's slug took him in the side and spun him halfway around.

At almost the same time Schrank's shotgun fired—both barrels at once, just like before—and the tall man was cut nearly in two.

A skinny fellow with a black bandana tied at his throat took a shot in Del Schrank's direction. It was a bad decision. And the last he would ever make. Longarm knocked him down with a bullet square over his heart. That one would not be getting up again.

Another shot sounded from the direction where Schrank was and the third man dropped to his knees. He recovered and aimed his pistol off to Longarm's right, presumably at Schrank. Longarm could not allow his prisoner to be killed, so he shot the man in the temple. His hat flew off and sailed a good ten feet in the air. The man who had been wearing it hit the ground long before the hat did.

"Are you all right, Del?"

"I am. How 'bout you?"

"Fine, thanks."

"Did you know this damn shotgun lets off both barrels at once?"

"Yeah, it did the last time too."

"You should've told me."

"Sorry. It slipped my mind."

While he had been jawing, Longarm was reloading his Colt. It was not something he had to consciously think about, and the movements came easy from long habit. After all, a man in his line of work did not want to be caught with an empty revolver or one even partially so. A full cylinder can make the difference between life and death.

The scene around them was a bloody mess. In addition to the dead men, the buggy horse was dead in its traces, hit by at least half a dozen errant rounds. Tim Brightson would have to submit a request to compensate him for his loss. Eventually he might even be paid. Longarm would certainly endorse the request.

"I think that will stop the bounty threat," Schrank said, stepping into view near the head of the slope above the ford.

"How's that, Del?"

Schrank pointed to the bodies on the ground. "This one over here is Luke Jennings. This one is Dag Taylor. Dag was the number two man in the gang. And that one over there is Charlie Watte. With Luke gone, there won't be a gang any longer."

"What about your friend Matt?"

Schrank sighed. "I'll testify to what I know. If that's what you want, that is."

"It ain't me that wants any of it, Del. That sort o' thing

will be up to the lawyers back in Denver. All I want is to get
you there safe an' sound, and with Jennings an' his crew
dead, there shouldn't be any trouble about that." He raised
his voice. "Unless you want to cause it, you sorry little cock-
sucker."

"What?"

"Not you, Del. Him!" Longarm pointed to a low shrub
off to one side where half a pale face could be seen hidden
in the foliage.

"Stand up, you piece of shit, or I'll put a bullet right
square between your miserable eyes."

"No, don't. Please. I'm . . . I'm not armed."

"Stand up."

Ron Jellicoe rose to his knees and then fully upright.

"Hold your hands up. Higher, you prick. Turn around.
Now lift your coat so's I can see the back o' your belt an'
britches."

Jellicoe did as he was told.

"I gave you a break once," Longarm reminded him.
"There won't be another. You went and fetched the Jennings
crew, you little weasel. You tried to get me and Del killed.
You'll spend time behind bars for that." Longarm scowled.
"Maybe I can talk the district attorney into sending you down
to Yuma to serve your time. Yuma is a son of a bitch. I'd say
you deserve Yuma, Ronnie."

"No, I . . . I can't go to prison. Really. I can tell you . . . I
can tell you lots of things. I can tell you who robbed the
Warren City Bank two months ago. I can tell you lots of
stuff like that."

"You want t'know the actual truth, Ronnie? I don't give a
shit about them other things. I just want to see you in prison
for a very long time."

"No, please, I . . ."

Longarm shut him up with a smash of his pistol barrel

across Jellicoe's mouth. The fat man was spitting teeth and dripping blood while Longarm finished locking handcuffs on him.

Longarm looked at Schrank and said, "Gather those horses for us, will you, Del? We'll have to hitch up one of them to get us and the buggy back to the railroad. And this sorry son of a bitch too, though given a choice I'd just as soon shoot him here and be done with it."

"Sure thing, Longarm. I, uh, I want to thank you for trusting me all this while." Schrank unbuckled the gunbelt at his waist and tossed it onto the seat of the now useless buggy, alongside with the shotgun that was already there.

"You can ride with me anytime, Del. Anytime at all." Longarm smiled and went about collecting the firearms that had fallen along with the Jennings gang.

The bodies could go in the buggy too, he figured. He could chain Jellicoe there with them while he and Del Schrank rode astride in comfort.

Longarm was whistling while he did what had to be done. With any kind of luck he could be back in Denver in two days. Back in time, perhaps, to pay a call on that pretty little waitress at his favorite café.

"What are you smiling about?" Del Schrank asked.

"Oh . . . nothing," Longarm said with a grin.

Watch for

LONGARM FACES A HANGMAN'S NOOSE

the 385th novel in the exciting LONGARM
series from Jove

Coming in December!

LONGARM

GIANT-SIZED ADVENTURE FROM AVENGING ANGEL LONGARM.

BY TABOR EVANS

2006 Giant Edition:

LONGARM AND THE OUTLAW EMPRESS

2007 Giant Edition:

LONGARM AND THE GOLDEN EAGLE SHOOT-OUT

2008 Giant Edition:

LONGARM AND THE VALLEY OF SKULLS

2009 Giant Edition:

LONGARM AND THE LONE STAR TRACKDOWN

2010 Giant Edition:

LONGARM AND THE RAILROAD WAR

M456AS0510

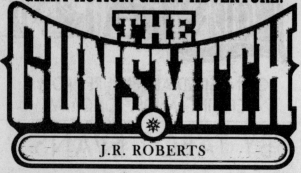

GIANT ACTION! GIANT ADVENTURE!

THE GUNSMITH

J.R. ROBERTS

Little Sureshot And
The Wild West Show
(Gunsmith Giant #9)

Dead Weight
(Gunsmith Giant #10)

Red Mountain
(Gunsmith Giant #11)

The Knights of Misery
(Gunsmith Giant #12)

The Marshal from Paris
(Gunsmith Giant #13)

Lincoln's Revenge
(Gunsmith Giant #14)

Andersonville Vengeance
(Gunsmith Giant #15)

penguin.com/actionwesterns

M455AS0510

DON'T MISS A YEAR OF

Slocum Giant
by
Jake Logan

Slocum Giant 2004:
Slocum in the Secret
Service

Slocum Giant 2005:
Slocum and the Larcenous
Lady

Slocum Giant 2006:
Slocum and the Hanging
Horse

Slocum Giant 2007:
Slocum and the Celestial
Bones

Slocum Giant 2008:
Slocum and the Town
Killers

Slocum Giant 2009:
Slocum's Great
Race

Slocum Giant 2010:
Slocum Along
Rotten Row

M457AS0510